x   c.1

Clark, Ann Nolan

To stand against the
wind

To Stand Against the Wind

To Stand
Against the Wind

ANN NOLAN CLARK

The Viking Press, New York

First Edition
Copyright © Ann Nolan Clark, 1978
First published in 1978 by The Viking Press
625 Madison Avenue, New York, N.Y. 10022
Published simultaneously in Canada by
Penguin Books Canada Limited
Printed in U.S.A.
1 2 3 4 5 82 81 80 79 78

Library of Congress Cataloging in Publication Data
Clark, Ann Nolan, To stand against the wind.
Summary: A young refugee now living in the United States ponders his
memories of life in a Vietnamese village before and during the war.
[1. Vietnamese Conflict, 1961–1975—Fiction.
2. Vietnam—Fiction] I. Title.
PZ7.C5296To   [Fic]   78-5966
ISBN 0-670-71773-8
X
C. 1

To Miss Margaret Hickey
whose thoughtful acts make
stepping-stones around the world.

Acknowledgments

My thanks to all my friends—and there were many—who helped me write this book. Without their assistance this manuscript would not have been completed. My thanks also to Mr. Kah, Lac, the Tang family and other Vietnamese whom I met and who helped Mr. Kah correct any unclear or misleading material that crept into the manuscript. Research for this book took two years, during which time I had many meetings and discussions with Vietnamese people and did an enormous amount of reading. I also checked my facts with the book *Village in Vietnam* by Gerald Hickey (Yale University Press, 1964), given to me by Margaret Hickey.

The family in this book is a created one, but it is typical of a village family, and, to the best of my knowledge, the events I describe are factual and authentic.

A.N.C.

To Stand Against the Wind

PART 1 | One

THE BOY, Em, sat on a rickety bench at a long oil-cloth-covered table, watching a small electric bulb, almost ceiling-high, swing on its short cord. As it swung, its faint light flickered across the tabletop, making him think of a single lightning bug in the summer dusk at home. The boy watched it intently, without actually seeing it.

The room looked bare, although there were three people in it, not counting the young boy at the table. There was an old man, as withered and brown as a dried apple, with a wisp of white hair showing beneath his cloth turban, and a long wisp of white beard flowing down his chest, but the eyes were young and alert and piercing.

They saw everything inside the room and seemed to see beyond the room as well. The second person, an old woman, was like a tiny, dainty flower living past its bloom but still sweet with the fragrance of springtime. The girl working beside them was young, little older than the boy at the table, and tiny; her skin was a golden color, and she had an air of quiet security about her. They were busy, intent upon their work, but so quiet, so still that they left the impression of not being there. The room felt empty.

The furniture in the room was placed in neat patterns. Two couches with faded, torn upholstery and sagging springs were placed end to end on one wall.

Against another wall, in the place of honor, a small island of peace and beauty in an otherwise ugly, unfriendly room, stood the Altar of the Ancestors, an old, ornately carved table, bought at a secondhand store but now polished to mirror-brightness and holding an ancient brass incense burner and copper vases, bowls, and candlesticks. Delicate silk scrolls and rice-paper posters with Vietnamese characters painted in red, yellow, and black hung on the wall behind the Altar—poems and proverbs written through the centuries by poets now present only in spirit. Some of the scrolls were as sturdy as if they had been painted only yesterday, but the parchment and silk of the very old ones looked thin and worn, as if any gentle wind could blow them into nothingness.

The boy's grandmother broke the stillness of the room. "Em, Grandson, the dawn is only a short time away, and then the candles must be lighted."

For a second the boy seemed not to hear her, his eyes

still on the swinging light bulb. Then he glanced out the window, and although he could not see the sun, he saw the patch of sky, yellow with the promise of day. He reluctantly went to the Altar of the Ancestors. There were no sweet-smelling joss sticks sending up their offering in the spirits of smoke as there should have been, no palm leaves or fern, and the flower vases were filled with artificial flowers. He lighted the incense in the age-old burner and sniffed at its unfamiliar odor. Would the ancestors, who were to be the family's guests in the house for this day, accept incense that did not smell like the incense of Vietnam? he wondered. He stood bent over the burner, sniffing and worrying, until thin blue lines of smoke rose, as it always had done. Then the boy was satisfied. The smoke was the spirit of prayers, shared, rising to meet their guests. The Day of the Ancestors had begun well. This day honored those who had gone centuries ago and especially those dear ones who had entered the Spirit World a year ago this day. They were being welcomed back to the world with the rising of the blue smoke of incense.

Em turned to the row of candlesticks, velvet-looking from years of reverent handling, and began to light each candle slowly, calling each one by a person's name, and seeing again each person as he had seen him in life. One, two, three, four, five, six, he named, lighting a candle and bringing back to memory their faces, their words, their ways. There were two more candlesticks, but instead of candles they held flowers, real flowers, bought at a flower shop with long-saved pennies. Em looked at his grandmother, and tears filled his eyes. He knew why these were flowers instead of candles. He knew they were not for blood kin, but for two greatly loved ones who were gone into the Spirit World of the Ancestors and who were missed and grieved for. His grandmother knew how much he loved them, and she had given them a place of dignity on the Altar. He touched the flowers in the candlesticks, but he could not call them by name. Which name would he say first? He loved them, they were part of him, bound to him with bindings stronger than kinship. He stood touching the petals of the fast-wilting flowers, remembering. He wanted to remember them, he thought; he would remember them always. If only he could do it without so much pain! "Is there some way," he asked silently, "that I could put my memories of you in a box and take them out only on days like this, instead of living them again and again in the black hours of the night?" There was no answer. He knew there would be no answer.

Candlelight flickered. Blue smoke rose. Morning light flooded through the narrow window. The girl, his older sister, Chi-Bah, turned off the electric light switch. The small cost for electricity must be saved. His sister's gesture made Em forget his grief for a second, and he turned his eyes to the pencil sharpener hanging by the window. Old Uncle had found it at the dump and brought it home and repaired it. It was Grandmother's joy to sharpen any pencil she could find, but it was Chi-Bah's worry that the old woman wasted so many pencils—which also cost money. Em turned from the Altar. No emotion showed in his face. His position in the family would not permit him to show his pain. Dry-eyed, he walked back to the table.

The two women were kneeling on mats placed on the floor at the foot of the Altar, their hands folded, their heads bent low, almost touching the floor. Grandmother looked up questioningly as her grandson sat again at the table. She reached over to nudge Old Uncle, who knelt apart from the women, and pointed to Em, who was now bending over a notebook. Old Uncle looked irritated at being roused so suddenly from his prayer of welcome to the ancestral guests, who were on their way for the yearly visit. He said abruptly, "He goes to write his memories of our loved ones who visit us this day."

Grandmother said, "He has no parchment, and writing on silk is a forgotten art. We have no rice paper. How can he write his memories without proper paper?"

"Memories," Old Uncle answered, "are written in the heart and mind. What does it matter the material on which they are recorded?" Old Uncle bowed his head, turning slightly from his elder sister, but Grandmother nudged him again—not so gently this time.

"Is he writing them in verse? Is he going to be a poet?"

Old Uncle looked at her, shaking his head. "Verse is painted with ink or water paint. What Em writes is written with the tears he has not shed. What does it matter?"

Grandmother nodded. She understood. She, too, bowed again before the Altar. Old Uncle, Grandmother, and Elder Daughter knelt in a silence that would wrap them until the day was finished.

Em bent over his notebook. He would write his memories; he would write them slowly with deep thought and loving care. Then he would put them in a box that Sam had given him and that he had brought with him to this place, their new home. We never call our new home by its rightful name, he thought, but always "this place" or "our new house." In Vietnam they had always talked about it and how someday they would come here. Now that they were really here it seemed that if they called its name the charm would be broken and they would not be here. He supposed it was for the same reason that they did not praise a new baby at its birth—for fear some evil would happen to it.

Em's thoughts returned to the record he intended to write. It would be for his children, who would probably never see Vietnam and would never know, unless he wrote about it, what their country had been like and what had happened to it and thousands of its people.

Grandmother could keep silent no longer. She came over to look at his paper, which had as yet no writing on it. "Is the record to be invisible?" she asked. "A blank piece of paper hanging beside the parchment, silk, and rice-paper scrolls?"

Elder Daughter looked up from her place at the Altar. "Grandmother, dear old one, the boy must think it first, and then the writing will come."

"Elder Daughter is correct," Old Uncle said slowly. "This is a day of meditation, when each one listens to what his heart tells him."

Grandmother patted Em gently to show him she meant well and that she loved him. The boy looked up at her. He understood and returned her love. He bent low over his tablet and wrote in the middle of the first line: "Our Land." Then he stopped writing and let memory flow out of his heart.

8

Two

BEAUTIFUL COUNTRY of the Land of the Small Dragon, rich delta of the Mekong River, home of his people for uncounted centuries—South Vietnam! Em closed his eyes, remembering the lovely land that was no more, letting the memories take possession of his heart, his mind, his senses. South Vietnam—he saw it again. He could smell its perfumes. He could feel it in body and spirit. Not as he had seen it at the last, the villages burned and the great trees felled, the ground bulldozed, the bridges wrecked, the dike walls broken, the roads torn up. He remembered it when it still had been beautiful.

He could see again the slow-moving river carrying its heavy burden of silt to enrich the little rice paddies of the land. He could see the great bridge spanning it like a bamboo arch. He could see the young rice plants in the paddies, the delicate green sprays encased in filigrees of gold. There is no other green like new rice plants, Em thought—a green with yellow overtones, as if it were being caressed by the sun's warm fingers. He saw it clearly, the paddy land of yellow-green rice plants swaying in rhythm with the lapping river waters and the network of man-made canals. Water and land were so flat that they looked almost on a level, a broad expanse of green and brown. The flatness of the water and the paddies was broken by clusters of green, thrusting upward into a flat blue sky, the bamboo, coconut palm, jack trees, and fruit trees which marked the small groups of houses where the rice-growers lived. At the edge of the delta was the swampland, and farther back the jungle, mysterious and dark, holding well its swamp holes and jungle-tangled tunnels, its secrets.

Few rice-growers ventured into the jungle depths; Em's people were not hunters. They were rice-growers, rice millers, and rice merchants. The very young and the very old were the gleaners, collecting every precious grain that was left after the harvest. Although the people gathering the harvest were careful and spilled few grains, the gleaners followed them, picking each fallen seed from the paddy mud, handling it as if it were a pearl of great value—which it was if a bad year followed with threatening famine. The jungle was full of many kinds of wild animals, but the people never hunted them, and although there were fish in the river and the canals, there were few commercial fishermen. Boys and men went fishing when fish was needed for food. Most families had twin fish ponds near their houses. Men or boys working as a team emptied the water from one pond to the other with tightly woven baskets, and fish left in the emptied pond were caught by hand. The people were farmers of the land and had been for centuries—growing, harvesting, and marketing. Rice was their way of life. They held the land in reverence. It nourished them in life. It cradled them in death.

Holding his pencil tightly, looking blindly at the paper on the table, Em could smell the rich odors of the land he had known so well. He could smell the delicate perfume of rice in flower, the heavy sweetness of golden rice at harvesttime. He smelled the clinging, heavy perfume of orchid and jasmine, fern and flowering vines and fruit trees in bloom. He smelled the scum of the swamp, the mildew of the jungle, the heat of the humid land in dry season and the cold wetness of the monsoon rains. Each smell had its own special place in the land he did not want to see again and could never forget.

When he was very little—or so it seemed now—his land had been a quiet land and his people a quiet people. The jungle animals kept themselves hidden in the jungle. The bird songs were so much a part of the setting that they could have been color instead of sound. The natural noises of people living together seemed united in one soft murmuring.

As Em had grown older, he had become aware of unrest among the people. The Vietnamese had always resented foreign domination—Chinese and later French—but they had always fought bitterly among themselves as well. They were patriotic, but their loyalty was to the land rather than to the people. Local elected officials and many secret societies and committees and factions had always existed side by side. Finally the country became divided into Northern communists and Southern noncommunists. In the South there were some sympathizers of the communists, and in the North of noncommunists. Then in the South there were the Vietcong, who were sympathetic to the Northern communists. All this was very confusing to Em then, and it was confusing to him now.

Em could remember that there were some families who still had friendly feelings for the French who had ruled them for about a hundred years. There was also still some Chinese influence in their culture, although many denied it. Finally, there were the guerrillas who hid in the swamplands of the delta and in the jungle bordering it. There had always been guerrillas. It was by guerrilla fighting that the people had been able to free their country from the Chinese—striking and hiding, then striking in a new location. That was their method of fighting, the way they had fought for a thousand years. It was their concept of war: crack and crumble the enemy bit by bit.

Now as he sat at the table in the quiet room, Em remembered the monsoon season, with its cold winds and welcome rains. He could feel the rain on his body as he worked in the fields, mending the earthen embankments that held the water in the paddies or the holes in the dikes of the canals. He could hear the rain at night, plopping on the thatched roof of his house. He could smell its damp cleanness and recall his delight that it had come at the right time for the growth of the rice. He loved the rainy season. It was so much more bearable than the searing heat of the dry land and the heavy humidity of the dry months. And yet he loved the dry months too. He was used to heat.

Em could feel the mud in the footpaths and the paddies. The mud was thick, soft, shin-deep, closing around his legs and sucking his feet downward as he waded through it. He did not mind the mud. It was part of the cycle of growth. Mud in the paddies at the right time of year meant rice in the stomach after harvesttime. There was nothing as precious as rice. It made life possible. As the rich silt of the Mekong River enriched the delta, so the delta nourished the rice that fed the people. One of their Ancients had said, "A grain of rice is like a drop of blood," and the people believed this. They repeated it to each other, keeping it always in mind. They taught it to the children, keeping it in their hearts: "As precious as a drop of blood."

Along the banks of the great curving river were the sprawling villages, each one consisting of many small, isolated hamlets. Em knew everyone in his own hamlet, but few in any of the other hamlets.

The hamlets were made up mostly of related families, and the few who were not blood kin were considered part of the family group. There was great family love and loyalty; kin ties were very strong, and so were ties with the extended family, which reached beyond the kinship bond. Strangers, however, or foreigners—people one did not know or trust—were treated with fear and suspicion. Except Sam.

When Em had been very young, he had thought of his hamlet as a peaceful garden. Each small thatched house surrounded by its high bamboo hedge had fruit trees, flowers of every size and shape and color, and the kitchen garden—the garden of vegetables grown mostly for the family food supply. If there was a surplus, it was taken to the Chinese market town of Cholon, between Saigon and the delta edge. The kitchen gardens were the women's domain. That was where they worked and chatted together, gossiped and complained. There was always a shelter for the water buffalo. Em shook his head. He couldn't think of that now. Not yet.

In the center of the hamlet, with the houses scattered around it, was the *dinh*, Temple to the Holy Ones of the community, the place for holding sacred objects and official documents, and the meeting place for the people. Often it was used as a school for the small children in the primary grades. There were also pagodas, temples built to the memory of some Ancients, and many tombs, the resting places for the ancestors.

Old Uncle, Grandmother's youngest brother and the hamlet scholar and poet, used to say, "When a man lives, he must have a home. When he dies, he must have a tomb. His bones must be returned to the land that nourished him so that his spirit will be at peace with his ancestors."

And the people of the hamlet nodded and said, "An old parchment is treasured for the words of wisdom inscribed on it." This was the way the hamlet people thought of Old Uncle.

The old man also knew a lot about the stars. He would

say, "A star that shines exceedingly bright at the time of a child's birth will foretell his destiny throughout his life." Em knew his star—Old Uncle had pointed it out to him—but it was to Old Uncle, not Em, that the star revealed its secrets. Old Uncle could point out the exact spot on which a new building should be erected so that the spirits, who considered the site their property, would not be disturbed. All the people of the hamlet brought their problems to Old Uncle, listened to his advice, and agreed with what he said—all but Grandmother. Old Uncle's sister listened and argued, but her arguments were to no avail. Old Uncle would be in meditation and would not know she was talking to him.

That was in the old days in Vietnam, Em thought, where Old Uncle had been the authority and had been confident about the rightness of what he said. Lately, in his new home, he had become more gentle and in some ways, perhaps, a little confused. About the stars, for instance. He said to Em, "There are no stars where we are now, or at least I can't see them. How can I be expected to hear what they tell me or to point yours out to you? You knew your star when you were in Vietnam. Why can't you find it here?"

In other ways he had changed, too. He had never planted anything in Vietnam. He was a scholar and a poet. He had said, "I work with words and thoughts, not with plants." But here, in this place, he had planted flowers in the sandy yard of their rented home. His fingers did what his failing eyes could not. They seemed to see as well as to feel. His hands knew from the feel of the dirt what each plant needed to make it grow.

Here the children who lived nearby loved him and followed him everywhere, guiding him gently because they knew he could see so little. Old Uncle trusted them and sang them songs he used to sing in Vietnam. Sometimes he would regain his old sparkle. Then the children's mothers began to bring him seeds and plant cuttings, and finally the fathers, coming home from work, stopped to admire his garden and told him in their language how wonderful it was to see flowers in the early spring, and the old man thanked them in Vietnamese, never admitting his knowledge of English.

Old Uncle had been Em's teacher, and although they were far apart in years, they felt very close to each other and shared respect and affection. Em had thought about asking advice from Old Uncle about writing his memories of Vietnam. Then he remembered why they had come to America. He remembered the responsibility that tradition had put on his shoulders. He must carry on the family name and honor. He must not run like a baby to the third uncle on his mother's side, asking him to help do what he should do. He was the Elder Son now. He was head of the house. He must make the decision himself.

Em sighed. "Thinking of all these things is too hard, because I must think about them before I can write them," he said to himself. "It is too hard. I cannot do it. But I must do it. I must leave a record for my family who come after me."

The small boy looked at his sister, who was polishing the incense pot. He looked at Old Uncle, deep in meditation. He looked at the pencil in his own hand. Em closed his eyes and bent over his tablet. He would need to hurry this remembering. When had it started? What had begun it? He knew the ending, but what was the beginning? "Father," he prayed, "wherever you are, come find me. Come help me do all these things that are too hard for me to do."

Three

I N THE HAMLET OF Em's village the houses were alike except in size, and some were built of different materials. Em's house had been one of the larger ones, and because of its size it had been built of planed lumber brought down the river by boat. The lumber had been made into a frame for the house by the man from upriver who had brought it and who was a carpenter. The roof was of thatch, and the walls and partitions were made of mats that had been woven by Mother and Grandmother. These mats were made of reeds that grew on the edges of the swampland and were sold by the bunch. The long reeds cost more than the shorter ones, but they made better-looking mats. The smaller houses in the hamlet had been built by the people who were to live in them, and they were made of logs and branches and palm fronds—anything at hand that could be collected and used. The outside walls and room partitions, like those of the larger houses, were made of mats that had been woven by the women. All the roofs were thatched. The water buffalo had their own huts, which were attached to the houses of their owners.

The houses were built on earthen embankments to keep the water out during the rainy season. Em's house, like almost all the others, had deep tunnels dug under the floor, and several underground rooms with hidden entrances. In these rooms were the family's most valued possessions, buried in clay jars—money, jewelry, sacred documents and objects that the family wanted kept safe.

Large or small, the houses were alike inside. There was a large main room where the Altar of the Ancestors had the most important place. On it were kept burnished copper bowls for flowers, incense, food, and rice wine. Each family also had its Ancestral Tablet made of delicate rice paper, on which were inscribed the names of the family's ancestors. Em's family held theirs in great esteem because it held the names of ancestors going back six generations.

All these names were cherished, respected, and honored from time to time by an age-old ritual. Called the Day of the Ancestors, it was a ceremony held for someone in the family who had recently died. For two days the family dressed in mourning clothes and recited prayers before the Altar. The head of the family performed a special ritual, which ended with the burning of the mourning clothes the family had worn. This was the way it had always been done. It was never changed—a tradition of centuries.

Em remembered that on one Day of the Ancestors anniversary his father had said to him and to Anh-Hai, his Elder Brother, "Six generations of our family rest in the earth of this hamlet—this hamlet that has been ours and will be ours for generations to come. Six generations, each father, son of his father, and father of his son, a continuing line of fathers and sons, all following the Will of Heaven, which brings tranquillity of heart and mind and soul. My father leaves his land to me as it was left to him and as I leave it to you, not as an individual possession but in trust, as the name and the honor of the family are left in trust."

This was a long speech for his father to have made, for he had been a quiet man of few words. Yet with those few words he could be gentle or stern, as the situation required. He was a man of many proverbs and had taught them to his sons by endless repetition. Em remembered that although he had been a quiet man he was always ready for laughter or a song he knew from his younger days.

His father had often talked to him, when they were alone, of the importance of the family and the name it bore. "There must always be a son to bear sons to keep the name in existence," he had said. He often repeated the words of the ancient wise ones of the Land of the Small Dragon. "I believe," he told him, "that training a son is accomplished by the good example of the father, and I expect my sons to imitate me in all ways as I have imitated your grandfather."

Both sons were like their father in small as well as important ways. Em especially tried to be like him. Once his sister had teased him. "You make the same gestures," she had said. "You pull your earlobe when you are thinking, and you like to laugh." Em had denied it, but secretly he was pleased.

"The boy is deep. He is serious," Old Uncle said one day, not knowing Em was listening.

"Yet he is happy," Mother had answered. "When the children quarrel, Em's laughter makes us peaceful again."

The father was a rice-grower, as those who had gone before him had been throughout their days. Father was proud of a good harvest. He tenderly cared for the young rice plants and was careful to protect his paddy. But some years when the rice harvest had been a poor one, when times were hard, when there had been too much rain or too little or it had come too soon or too late, Father had gone to nearby Saigon to work as a mechanic. He had always loved automobiles, trucks—anything that had a motor. He treated every screw and bolt and nut as if it were a rice seedling, and he seemed to know instinctively where each bolt and screw belonged and why and how it functioned.

Thinking of his father, Em felt hot tears sting his eyes. The boy bent his head lower over his tablet. He must not cry. "Father," he whispered, "where are you? Is your spirit at peace in your loved Vietnam, or does it wander homeless and lost without a resting place in the hamlet where you were born? Father, you know I love you very much. I try to be like you. Could your spirit come to me just long enough to tell me what is right for me to write in the record?" Sometimes Em felt his father's spirit very close to him, but other times it seemed to be nowhere, not to exist. "Father," the boy said softly, so no one could hear him, "Father, I need you very much." Cautiously the boy touched his eyes. They were wet, but no tears had fallen from them.

Em looked up. Old Uncle was looking at him. He silently looked at the paper where nothing had been written. "If you only understood," the boy wanted to tell him, but no words came. "I have to get it straightened out in my mind before I can write about it. Please, Respected Old One, what you want me to do I cannot do." Old Uncle looked as if he might be willing to listen to anything Em had to say, but when the boy said nothing, the old man again became lost in meditation.

Em pictured the house in Vietnam. That would not hurt as much as remembering his father. At home, first in importance was the Altar of the Ancestors, which took up a large part of one wall. In front of the Altar were woven mats where the hamlet's honorable men were often asked to sit and meditate concerning the Ancestral Virtues. Em saw them now, small, wraithlike old men, their heads covered in folded-turban fashion, their long, thin whiskers, their wrinkled golden skins, and eyes that looked with tranquillity into the beyond that they knew not and yet were part of.

Here in this new home, in this new country, Em thought, his family had its Altar of the Ancestors in their rented house, but there were no old men sitting meditating. There were a hundred or more Vietnamese refugees scattered about the town, but they met only at church-sponsored parties at which meditation was unknown. A few families got together by themselves occasionally, but not often. They were scattered in family groups throughout the town, and most of them had not known one another before coming here.

As for Old Uncle, he seldom meditated any more. He was busy from sunrise until dark coaxing the flowers in the sandy yard to grow big and strong. He sang to himself as he worked and recited all the old Vietnamese classics by heart to the children who followed him around. They thought he was singing them special songs even when he was only talking. Old Uncle was happy. He brought laughter back to Em, and the two were as close and dear to each other as they had been in Vietnam.

The boy's mind went back to the hamlet house again. At the back of the main room dried bricks of paddy were stored, along with the handmade implements for rice-growing. Hand tools hung from the rafters, and hanging shelves made of palm fronds held wooden bowls and clay pots. There were narrow, hard plank beds everywhere, and hammocks.

The kitchen was second in importance to the Altar of the Ancestors, and where to place it was a question that took much thought and advice from the hamlet scholars who had knowledge of such things. It had to occupy the north or northwest portion of the house. In it, in addition to three or four earthen braziers, was the stove, which consisted of three flat stones. These stones were the three

Spirits of the Hearth. Nothing must disturb or anger them. They were the heart of the home. If the Hearth Spirits were in harmony, the family was in harmony. Harmony brought tranquillity, and tranquillity was every man's desire.

Thinking back now, Em remembered the kitchen as a place of good smells. It seemed, as he thought about it, that his mother or grandmother was always cooking. Although they worked in the kitchen garden and, when needed, in the rice paddy, he remembered them best in the kitchen, cooking.

Most days when Em was hungry, he ate a bowlful of rice and fish sauce, and salt anytime and anywhere hunger made its wants known to him. But when his family sat eating together, the boy always sat beside his grandmother, who fed him tasty bits of fish, nuts, vegetables, and fruit from the bowls set before her place. Of the four children of her son's family, he, the youngest, was her favorite—aside, of course, from the respect and honor she gave Anh-Hai, the Elder Son.

Chi-Bah, the Elder Daughter, was a year younger than Anh-Hai. She was the beauty of the family, small and dainty and gentle.

Thu, Daughter Number Two, was three years younger than Chi-Bah and three years older than Em, as his family called him. Thu was very much like her grandmother. Em remembered her now as always busy, always running here and there, and always talking. "Too much talk for a girl," Old Uncle would say sadly. "Girls should not talk, they should listen, ready to obey." Thu respected Old

24

Uncle and honored his age, but she rarely listened to what he had to say.

Grandfather was a silent, happy, tranquil man. Em had never seen anyone with such tranquillity of heart. Rice-growing was his life. He tended the crop from seedling to harvest. When he was not working his paddy fields, he prayed and meditated. All his large family had been girl children, except the one son, Em's father. Grandfather had raised his son well, Em thought. The son was a good and honorable man. And now that Grandfather's son had two sons of his own, the family name would continue. It would go on for the next generation and, Heaven willing, for generations to come, and its honor would be steadfast. Grandfather had the small plot of land where their home and their rice fields were located. The old man did not feel that he owned this land as an individual, but that it was in his keeping for the family of the future. At his death it would pass on to his Elder Son, as his son would pass it on to *his* son. It was not a possession; it was a responsibility that was carried with concern and pride by the head of the house. Grandfather loved the land and knew he would hand it on to those who would serve and protect it.

When the rice was harvested, Father often went to Saigon to work for a week or two or a month or two, depending on how much money the family needed at the time. Saigon, or part of it, was a beautiful city of wide tree-shaded streets, lovely parks, elaborate houses, and ornate public buildings. The French, homesick for their own country, had called it the Paris of the Orient. Father had never gone to Paris in France, but he was impressed by what he heard of it, and he liked Saigon. "Not as a place to live one's life," he would explain, "but to know it as a city where one can work and know one's way about."

Em remembered that when Anh-Hai, the Elder Son, was about ten years old, Father decided to send all the children to school in Saigon. "Although I have no great love for the French, who tried for so long to govern us," he told Grandfather, "they have a certain elegance of manner, and certainly my children should know as much as the French know." Grandfather nodded but said nothing. Father tried to strengthen his argument. "As you know, French is our second language. The children should go to a French school." All the answer Grandfather gave was a shrug of his shoulders. Although Father was not entirely satisfied, he decided this decision was agreeable to Grandfather.

Father also decided that Mother should go with the children to make them a proper home, and also himself when he was working in Saigon. They would come home weekly and at all festival occasions. That way, they would remain hamlet people in their hearts. After much thought Father decided that Em should stay with his grandparents and Old Uncle. Father said, "Em is too young. He must first become rooted in the hamlet pattern of living so that he can learn new ways but not necessarily accept them."

Mother did not want to go to Saigon, nor did she want to take the three older children with her. She thought the hamlet school was good enough. The children did not need an outward polish of French manners. And she did not want to leave Em with the three old people. If she had to go to Saigon, she wanted Em with her—but no one asked her what she wanted to do. She had been taught that as a girl she obeyed her father, as a woman she obeyed her husband, and if he died, she obeyed her oldest son.

Em had not wanted to go to Saigon to school. He wanted to stay at home with his friends. When the day's work was over, he wanted to go swimming in the canals or fishing in the river in his father's pirogue at sunset. As for school, Em knew that Old Uncle still had a great deal more to teach him. Thu, the younger sister, did not want to go to Saigon, especially if Em was to be left behind. She had treated him as her doll and her baby since she had been old enough to carry him on her back while she was at work or play. He was her special responsibility and delight. Only Chi-Bah, Elder Daughter, wanted to go to Saigon. Ever since she could remember, she had wanted to be a typist and go to the wonderful country of America to type for an emperor or a king or whatever great man was there who would need to have his documents typed.

But no one asked them if they wanted to go or to stay in the hamlet. They were children, and they did what their father thought was right for them. So one morning they went to Saigon, leaving Em behind with his grandparents and Old Uncle. The family would walk part of the way and ride on the bus for the remainder of the trip. They carried all they would need in woven baskets tied to bamboo poles across their shoulders. There were no tearful good-byes. This was what their father thought was right, and so they accepted it as right.

At first Em missed them terribly; most of all, he missed Thu. She had been his constant companion for as long as he could remember. She had always been nearby when he needed her. Although Father had said they would come home to visit every week, many things happened that kept them in Saigon for three or four weeks at a time. They came for all the festivals and for rice planting and if they were needed for harvest, but each time they left, Em seemed to miss them more.

Then one day it was decided that Em was old enough to have the entire responsibility of the water buffalo.

Water buffalo are by nature tame, patient creatures, but Em's buffalo was, in addition, affectionate and responsive. The boy took him to graze early in the morning when it was cool and fresh. He found the shadiest place for the hot noontime rest and went with him to the river to swim or stand in the cool water. Em permitted the herons to walk on the huge animal's back and eat the insects that would otherwise plague the big, patient animal. Above all, Em loved his buffalo as he would have loved a dog if he had owned one. The buffalo was his responsibility, his pet, and his companion. His heart hurt now as he thought how much he missed the gentle creature.

And he missed Sam. Whenever he thought of his buffalo, he thought of Sam, although they had not come into his life at the same time. The buffalo had been his friend many years before he had known Sam, but they had gone out of his life together, his two best friends. No one—

nothing—could take their place in his heart, he thought. No one—nothing—ever could. His two first friends.

Em rested his head on his folded arms. He was very tired. He had gone backward a long distance in space and time, and now he would have to think of all that had happened from then until today. There had been so many happy times that he could not remember all of them. Perhaps he would pick out a few of the happiest to write about—but there had been unhappy times, too, and he would need to think about them also. Remembering them would not be difficult. For almost a year he had been trying not to remember them. The year would end today. "Maybe if I remember all of them now, just sit here and remember them," he thought, "it will be like washing my memory clean. Maybe I will never need to think of them again."

Four

THE YEARS PASSED, but Em never went to school in Saigon. Every year Father said that this year would be a good time for Mother to take Son Number Three to Saigon to school. "There is still need for him to know the French language," Father would say, "and now that the French are leaving and the Americans are coming to help us run our government, there will be need for him to know the English language as well."

Silent laughter could be felt running in ripples around the family circle because Old Uncle, who was Em's teacher, was well-versed in French and could read and write in English, although he would not admit it. And he, as even Father must have known, was teaching both languages to his young people.

No one ever argued with Father or Grandfather. Mother and the children listened to what they said and felt that what they said was right. Old Uncle listened but, being a scholar and a poet, talked if he liked. Now he said, "Yes, that is a wise decision. If your Number Three Son stays much longer with me as his instructor, you will have another scholar in this small hamlet. He already knows by heart *The Tale of Kieu* which, as you know, is one of the world's greatest works of literature. He knows a thousand years of Chinese history and eighty years of French domination. He writes Chu Nom, the elegant Chinese writing of scholars, as well as Quôc Ngu, the national script of the common people. When he goes to Saigon, he will learn European ways and forget what I have taught him, which, of course," he added in a quiet way, "has no importance. It is indeed a wise decision." Em knew that when Old Uncle went out into the night to listen to the stars a moment later, he must have felt great contentment and peace, for he had not argued with Father. "If there is harmony in the house, there is well-being in the soul," he would have said to the night wind, and well-being would have risen up within him. Em knew life in the hamlet would be dull for his uncle if Em were to leave and go to school in Saigon. Old Uncle did not intend to live a dull life; Em knew that too.

Inside the house Grandmother said to her daughter-in-law, "If my son sends my youngest grandson to Saigon and you take him there, you will have taken away the life of this house and the sunshine in the hearts of three old, tired people—but you must obey your husband. Take the boy to Saigon and let us die with no laughter to light our way to the Spirit World."

Silence greeted Grandmother's words. Father and Grandfather pretended not to hear her. She was only a woman. They would be told by some greater authority what was right to do.

After a time Grandmother spoke again, this time to her husband. "Today I saw a young buffalo," she said, as if not a word had been spoken about sending her favorite grandchild away. "I hope the man will be willing to sell it to you."

Grandfather was startled. "We have a buffalo," he told her, "a good, strong one. Why should we want to buy another one?"

Grandmother seemed surprised at Grandfather's question. "You know, of course—everyone knows—that when my youngest grandson goes to Saigon, his buffalo will sadden and die. That buffalo follows him around like a younger brother. He will never understand why his young master has forsaken him, but I'm sure you can replace the poor creature with this young buffalo I saw today." Silence greeted these words also.

Soon Grandmother went to bed. Em could see she felt pleased with herself. She had set an example for her daughter-in-law and her grandchildren; she had shown them she was ready to obey her husband and his son even though it meant the sacrifice of a strong and good buffalo.

After Grandmother had gone, Grandfather said, "The

young one we have been talking about gives promise of becoming the best rice-grower in the delta. Already he guides the buffalo in drawing the plough through the mud of the seed beds at planting time. This is a man's work. No other boy in the delta has such mastery over his buffalo."

Father said, "I have never heard of a water buffalo dying because it was forsaken, but who knows why a buffalo dies? Let us sit in the moonlight and think about this. We are good men. We have followed the trail our ancestors made for us. Surely the Will of Heaven will be made known to you and to me."

Mother whispered to the hearthstones in the kitchen where the House Spirits rested, "I accept what must be accepted."

Em remembered that he had gone outside to comfort his buffalo and to tell him, "My father is always right. I know he will tell me that I am to stay here with you."

His father did tell him he had to stay for another year in the hamlet where he had been born. And so it had been for all the years. Every year there was the discussion and then at last the decision, and Em never went to Saigon to school.

The years that followed were quiet and filled with joy. Old Uncle liked teaching him, Em could tell. Grandfather liked working the rice paddy with him, and Grandmother never tired of all their laughter. The hamlet was like a hidden cove of still and bright water.

It was different in the cities and ports and market towns of the rest of Vietnam. True, almost all the French were gone, but the North and South were arguing bit terly. The Vietcong were siding with the North. Powerful nations were giving aid to the North while the military of the United States came to the South. At first they came to advise and train the Vietnamese. Here and there military bases were built. More and more Americans came. "The Americans," the people said. "The Americans have come."

Soon Americans—big, noisy, friendly young men—came to the villages and the hamlets. In the beginning the people of Em's hamlet were afraid of the strangers. They were so big, so very big. The children were the first to make friends with them. Em could see that the Americans liked children and that the children knew it. They followed the men, and the men gave them chewing gum and candy and teased them and played ball with them and walked around, looking at everything and asking questions.

It was at about this time that Em met Sam. Em had seen him often. From the very first Sam had seemed to be someone special. This puzzled Em. He did not know why. Sam was tall and thin with big feet and big hands and a big nose, but many of the Americans were that way. Em noticed that Sam was quiet. In that way he was different. Many of the Americans were noisy and full of laughter. Sam did not talk much or laugh often, but when he did laugh, his laughter was joyful and delighted Em. Sam was friendly to all the boys who followed him around, giving them candy and bubble gum. Em remembered now that he had hated the bubble gum. It made him feel sick when the giant balloon of gum popped from his mouth like the distorted prey a wild animal was eating. He had liked the candy, but as his portions seemed to be mostly gum, he stayed out of the way while Sam was giving out his treats for the day.

Otherwise he was never far away from the young man. He watched Sam intently. He watched his every movement. He watched Sam look at everything and everybody and then think for a while and finally write in a little book he kept in his pocket. Em wondered if Sam could be a scholar and a poet like Old Uncle, but he thought not. Sam played ball, and he never seemed to sit and meditate. Sam was fun. Old Uncle was not.

But one day was different. Sam was sitting in the shade of a stately palm and meditating. He was not writing. He did not have his little book with him, but he was reading a bit of folded paper which he took out of his pocket, unfolded carefully like a thing of value, read slowly. Then he folded it and again placed it in his pocket and meditated, chewing stems of grass, which he spit out as if they were distasteful. Then he repeated the reading of the paper.

Em's water buffalo moved restlessly. He wanted Em to swim with him or sit on his back and play his flute or coax the herons to come eat the irritating insects. Em did nothing but sit, his eyes on a distant palm. Silently he began to creep toward the palm, and not a fern or a leaf or a stem of grass moved as he crept nearer. Finally he was directly behind Sam, sitting on his haunches and trying to read the paper Sam read so slowly. The writing was clear but too small for Em to read. After what seemed an eternity of fruitless effort the boy gave up.

"Hi," he said. That was the American way of greeting.

Sam was clearly startled. He had not known anyone was within at least half a mile of him. But he took time to fold the paper carefully before returning the cheerful greeting. "Hi to you," he said. "So you know the famous word of friendly approach."

"Yes," Em agreed, "but I do not like it. A friendly approach should be longer and say more than just a sound that has little meaning."

Now Sam really looked startled. "So you speak English!"

"Oh, no," Em said seriously, thinking of Old Uncle, "I do not know English, nor do I speak it."

Sam was silent, then he asked, "What answer can I make to that?"

Em flushed, then he said, "Americans have names, don't they? What am I to call you?"

Sam answered as casually as he could, "Sam."

"Just Sam, no other name?" Em asked.

"Sam Fordman."

"Then I call you Fordman?"

"No. Fordman is my father's name. We use our individual names first and our fathers' names last."

Em thought this over for quite a while. Americans really were different, he thought. Finally he said, "My name that I write in records is Nguyan Van Laos."

"Do I call you Nguyan," Sam asked, "or perhaps Van Laos?"

Em had laughed and Sam had laughed with him. Em explained, "You call me Em. Em means one of the young ones. You see, there are three older than I. Anh-Hai is the Elder Brother Number Two. He is the oldest."

Then Sam asked, "Why isn't your Elder Brother Number One?"

Em was shocked, almost frightened. "Oh, no," he said quickly, "not One. Number One is too important. The Evil Spirits would be jealous and cause him harm. They must never know he is Number One. My Elder Sister is Chi-Bah. She is a year younger than Anh-Hai. We call her Chi-Bah, which means Elder Sister, because she is a girl." Then Em continued. "She is three years older than my next sister, whose name is Thu. Grandmother would not permit her to be called Em. She is too pretty. After a while we became used to calling her Thu."

"So it's to be Sam and Em," Sam said, extending his hand, which Em took graciously. Then Sam hurriedly hunted through his pockets, but not the one that held the folded paper. "I seem to be out of candy," he said, "but I have bubble gum."

"Thank you," Em replied, taking the gum, and then his eyes lighted with laughter. "And I have betel leaves. Have you had betel leaves?"

"Thank you," Sam said, taking the leaves. "What do you do with them?"

"Chew them," the boy said enthusiastically. "This will make your teeth black as night."

Sam tried to hide his feelings about this, but he failed. Em was delighted with the horror Sam showed. He let the situation dangle for a while and then he said, "It is permitted to exchange gifts if both are satisfied with the exchange."

Sam waited a reasonable time before he said, "I would reluctantly but happily exchange gifts if that is also your wish."

Em waited a still longer time and then said, "Yes, with many thank-you's and gratitude."

"And great appreciation," Sam added. The boy and the man broke into laughter and shared their delight in knowing that they understood each other: they were friends.

Now Em looked at the Altar of the Ancestors, wondering why it was that he and Sam had become friends so quickly, why long before he had spoken to Sam he had liked him. Usually this did not happen. Vietnamese people were suspicious of all strangers. They must know them a long time before they accepted them, and even then they might never really trust them. But he had trusted Sam. There must have been some reason for their friendship. It must have been written in the stars. Em looked down at the clear, blank pages of his tablet, still thinking of Sam.

Sam had said he was not in the military; he was a civilian, a reporter. He wrote for papers and magazines for the Americans at home to let them know how the Vietnamese were getting along in "This Thing." Sam never called it a training program or a war. He always called it "This Thing."

From that time on, Em spent every idle moment with Sam, and before long Sam was working with both Em and Grandfather in their paddy. Grandfather told his grandson to ask Sam why he was helping them. Sam answered, "This is my job, to get to know you so I can tell my people about you." The answer satisfied Grandfather. He accepted Sam as an honest man, and he was glad to have him work in the rice paddy.

Em took Sam to meet his water buffalo. "I think he likes you," Em said, feeling shy. "I think you've taken to each other."

Sam said seriously, "He's the best water buffalo I've ever met." Then Sam asked Em what he had been wanting to ask him for a long time. "How come you speak English? Who taught you?"

"Old Uncle, who is my teacher," Em replied.

"I want to learn the Vietnamese language. Do you think Old Uncle would teach me?"

"I don't know," Em said doubtfully. "I don't think he could because he does not speak or understand English."

"Then how could he have taught the language to you?" Sam wanted to know.

"I don't know, but he says that he never speaks it, only to me."

Sam smiled. "Let's go ask him."

Em was worried. How would Old Uncle treat Sam? he wondered. Sam was so wonderful, he thought. Em wanted everyone to like him. He was not sure that Old Uncle would. "He liked you," Em said later, "I could tell he liked you!"

"He's taken to me—just like your buffalo," Sam answered. It was the same with Grandmother. Sam liked her cooking, and this pleased her.

A few weeks later, when Mother and the children came home to visit, there was Sam, learning Vietnamese from Old Uncle, practicing the new language on Grandmother as he ate and praised her cooking, working with Grandfather and Em, and on friendly terms with the buffalo. Anh-Hai, Elder Brother, had almost finished school and had enlisted in the army and was waiting to be called to his government's service. He had many questions to ask the American, and although Sam was ten years older than Anh-Hai, a strong friendship was quickly established between them. Sam teased Chi-Bah and Thu, calling them the "little butterflies" and pretending he could not tell them apart. He told them he was going to take them back to America with him and say they were two little dolls he had found in the delta.

Now Em recalled that Father was the slowest and the last of the family to take Sam to his heart—but Father had had his mind on other matters in those days. He, too, wanted to enlist and do what he could to aid his government, but the rice paddy and the family were also his responsibility. Mother had looked upon Sam as another son, homesick for his own parents. He was an only child, which shocked Mother. Em knew she wondered if all American parents had only one child. She would think about this strange fact and about Sam when she took the children—all but Em—back to school in Saigon.

Times worsened. There was ground combat now. Bombing was carried out by Americans in American planes. Em and the other children in the hamlet soon learned to tell the planes apart and to know them by name. There were the B-52's that came so fast that one could hear them only as they flashed by, and the heavily armed helicopters, and the great jets that flew low over the land. The planes came in groups of a dozen or more, and bombing was mostly in the afternoon. At night there were flares dropped by parachutes to show the Americans where the enemy was, for the Vietcong seemed to be everywhere.

The people of Em's hamlet knew this. They knew that some of those who lived among them were Vietcong, and they suspected others were. The South Vietnamese feared the VC's, as the Americans called them, but for that very reason they often befriended them, although some did so through loyalty or out of confusion, not knowing what else to do. They refused to talk about them. Old Uncle warned Em not to ask questions or to answer them. The old man told him, "Know too much, die too soon." Em obeyed him. He did not talk or listen. He did not know.

Sam also had advice to give him. He told him again and again, "If you hear a plane coming, hide if you have time. Otherwise don't move. The order has gone out, 'Shoot anything that moves.' " Em understood. He had seen that those who moved died quickly, and he had obeyed Sam's warning.

It was exciting, he thought, but it was also confusing. Once when people he knew had been killed and others injured, he had asked Sam, "Why? Why is there war? Why is there fighting?"

Sam said, "This thing is as confusing to me as it is to you. Most of us don't know why we got into this mess and why we don't get out of it."

Old Uncle asked, "How do the other Americans feel about what's happening?"

Sam shrugged. "Some think we are doing right. Some

think this is your thing, you should fight it. We have no right to interfere."

Old Uncle still was not satisfied. "How do *you* feel about it?" he asked.

Sam looked at him before he spoke. Then he said, "I am a reporter. I come for facts. If I let my feelings enter in, they would color what I write. I write what I see."

Old Uncle was satisfied. He nodded, and for once he forgot that he did not speak English. He told Sam, "That is good. That is the right way to be a reporter."

For the first time, Mother complained about living in Saigon. She wrote to Father, "American money is ruining everyone, all of us. The Americans have money and throw it around, and our people, who do not have it, are greedy and take it. They sell everything that can be sold, and the Americans buy it. I want to come home to our safe, quiet hamlet. I want to bring the children home where their ancestors rest in peace and their spirits will guide and protect us."

Father was upset about the letter. He had never known Mother not to want to do what he had said was right. That night Old Uncle said, "Something is bothering the stars. I do not like what they tell me." He went outside. He wanted no part of the discussion about whether or not to permit Mother to bring the family home.

Em knew that Sam had found out many things about Vietnam, but he had not learned that one did not argue with Father, or perhaps, Em thought, he did not want to argue but he wanted Father to know, for now Sam said, "Let's go to Saigon and see what it's like. I need to go, and I can borrow an army jeep and take all of us."

42

Immediately Father said, "Yes. I have not been to Saigon for some time. I'd like to go."

And immediately Grandfather said, "No. I have not been to Saigon in years and I have no intention of going now."

Old Uncle came back into the house. "What is this I hear about going to Saigon?" he said. "I'd like to go."

"We will take Em, also," Sam said boldly, not knowing if Father would permit it. "He needs to see facts, so he will know." They all thought about what Sam had said.

Suddenly Grandfather spoke, and he spoke as a father does to his son. "What we need to know," Grandfather said, "is what is the right thing to do. There may be something there that we see that will be an omen of what it is that we should do."

Grandmother said nothing. Em knew she did not care if they went to Saigon or not. She would have liked to have gone, but Sam had learned their customs so well that even he had not asked her.

So it was decided. They would go to Saigon. Sam went off to borrow an American jeep. It took him two days, but when he came back they were ready to go. Grandfather sat in front with Sam. Em could see that as long as he had decided to go, he would be in command. Grandfather felt young again and eager.

Em remembered that the trip to Saigon had not been easy. In many places the road had been bombed and they had had to walk for a distance. The big bridge over the river, which had been their pride, was gone; almost nothing was left to show that a bridge had been there. They had had to ford the river. Grandfather stayed in the jeep with Sam. Em and the others swam, then pushed the jeep up the slippery bank on the far side. Several dikes of the canals had been destroyed, and the water running across the road had made mud holes deeper than any flooded paddy. They pushed the jeep—even Grandfather helped—while Sam drove it with all the power it had.

At last they reached Saigon. Father was shocked. He kept saying, "This cannot have happened. This cannot be real." Sam said nothing.

The streets were flooded with people, like water flowing; some with the current, some against it—the very old, the very young. There were mobs of jeering children, pushing, shoving, shouting, stealing. "These are the street people," Sam said. "They live in the streets. They have no place to go."

"They could go back to their hamlets," Grandfather said. Sam did not reply.

On every street corner Em saw beggars—the crippled, the blind, the peddlers. There were starving children lying on the sidewalks without the strength or the desire to move. There were those who had died since morning.

The Americans were everywhere, big and noisy, but now, Em remembered, they did not seem friendly, as they had when they had visited the hamlet. "I thought Americans were different," Em said to Sam. "Have they been this way always?"

"Many of them have changed," Sam answered. "This thing has changed them. Many, probably most of them, have not had as much money before with no way to spend it. Many of them are homesick and disillusioned. This Thing isn't what they thought it would be."

Old Uncle was quick to defend the Americans. "Well," he said, "it's a difficult thing to learn—that you kill or be killed."

Grandfather asked, "Which is worse?" No one answered him.

"I want to go home to my hamlet," Grandfather said, "and take my grandchildren with me."

"O.K.," Sam answered cheerfully in English. Then, speaking Vietnamese, "We will go home, but there are two other places I must visit, so I will take you with me."

Sam took them to an orphanage that housed the children who had no families left to take care of them. Em remembered how clean the place was, how few people there were to take care of the children, how terribly poor they seemed, and how brave. They passed by children, many of them Em's own age, standing silently in groups or by themselves, patient, hungry, cared for, but unloved. There were too few people and too much work for love to be given to so many children. Old Uncle wept, but he was a poet. Poets may weep, Em thought.

Em looked at the clock on the wall. It was getting late. He must hurry his remembering. His record must be written before the Altar candles burned low and the blue smoke from the incense pot curled upward. The record must hang on the wall beside the other poems as offering to those who had gone to the Spirit World and to those who would come afterward.

Em closed his eyes, and the pictures in his mind returned. Sam had taken them to a children's hospital. There seemed to be hundreds of children here—blind, hands and feet missing, bandaged with nothing but their dark eyes showing, neither knowing nor caring why they lived.

Em remembered he had been sick, and Sam had been worried, but Grandfather said sternly, "Let the boy vomit. It will relieve the pain in his belly if not in his heart."

He and Sam and Elder Brother had walked home. The jeep had been too full of belongings and Mother, her daughters, Old Uncle, and Grandfather. Father had driven. He could drive a jeep as well as a car. Em was proud of him. The jeep would pass them, and they would catch up with it and push it, and it would pass them again. It was a beautiful night. But overhead were the giant planes and the parachutes and the flares, and no one moved until all was quiet again.

Sam was talkative. "War," he said, "leaves scars."

Em was surprised. Sam had never used the word "war" before. Then he realized that Sam was talking about all wars, not just about "This Thing."

"Scars on the land and on the people, all the people, both sides, all ages. Scars are deep and ugly. They take a long time to heal."

Sam stopped talking while they pushed the jeep out of a mud hole. "In a couple of days I'll be leaving you for a week or so," he said. "I want to go up North to see for myself."

"Will you go in a jeep?" Em asked him.

"No, I'll fly in one of the planes, a jet maybe."

"You will come back?"

"Of course I'll come back." Sam laughed. "I must come back to help bring harmony to the family. I've a hunch that Chi-Bah is not too happy about coming home."

"No," Elder Brother replied. "She has finished her training and she wants to work for the Americans as a secretary. I also want to get in the army just as soon as I am called."

"Your father wants to enlist too," Sam said. "What do you want to do, young one?" he asked Em.

"I want to stay and wait for you."

He had stayed, Em remembered, and waited for Sam, and Sam had come back as he had promised.

Five

NOW THEY WERE all home together, all ten of them, counting Sam, who came as often as he could and stayed two or three days at a time. There was harmony in the home, but, Em remembered, things were not entirely right. Everyone seemed to have a grief eating his heart. He felt it, but he did not know what their hurts were, and this worried him so that he, also, was not filled with well-being.

"At last we are together after all these years you spent away from home permitting the children to get European ideas in that school in Saigon," Grandmother said as she stirred the pot, cooking over the three hearthstones that made the stove. "All of us should have stayed at home here in our small hamlet where we always have belonged and always will belong."

Em could tell Mother was annoyed at the remark because it was not she who had taken the three oldest children to Saigon. It had been Father's orders and Grandmother knew it, but Mother had been taught as a small child and later as a young girl that a wife paid great respect to a mother-in-law. Her only reply had been to chop more vigorously at the mound of vegetables on her chopping board.

Grandmother waited, hoping Mother would say something that would add a little spice to life. After a time she said, "All are home now, but it will be only for a short time."

Mother could agree with this. "Yes," she said sadly, "soon our oldest born, our Number Two Son, will be leaving for the war. I will miss him. It will be a real break in our family."

Grandmother bent over the pot, sniffing its contents, then testing it for taste with a small, bony finger. "My Oldest Grandson will not be the only one to go," she said in a satisfied voice, feeling that she knew more than Mother did. "My Oldest Son, your husband, is eating his heart out to be off to the war."

"I know," Mother said quietly. "He will make the right decision when he receives some sign directing him." Mother's voice was calm. She knew she could wait. She knew she could accept.

This time it was Grandmother who was annoyed. She had not known that her daughter-in-law had noticed her husband's deep uncertainty. She said, "All these years you have been a good wife. This much I say for you, but"—and the little old lady chuckled—"my Granddaughter Chi-Bah is now wearing her hair in a chignon like a young lady. What is her age, do you know?"

"Fifteen but soon to turn sixteen," Em's mother answered.

"Sixteen, seventeen is the right age for marriage," Grandmother said, "and it's my guess that the Matchmaker will be here at any time now to look us over."

Mother made no reply. To say that she, too, thought a matchmaker would come, and from what family, was not to be considered. This was not done in Vietnam. There must appear to be complete surprise when such an event happened.

Grandmother waited hopefully but, receiving no answer, said, as if to herself, "Some boy she met in that school in Saigon, I think. I hope he is from some other hamlet. This is as it should be."

Now Em smiled, remembering. He had been reading one of Old Uncle's books, sitting so quietly that his mother and grandmother had not known he was there, but although his eyes had been upon his book, his ears were open to the conversation. Now he spoke. "Is that right? Is she going to get married, do you think? It would be exciting for Chi-Bah to marry."

Both women turned in astonishment to look at him, but before they could speak, Thu, who had been resting in the hammock, said, "She hopes to get married. Every day she hopes the Matchmaker will come. Can't you tell? One day she is as happy as a singing bird and the next day as stormy as a monsoon cloud."

Grandmother was pleased. She had hoped that something would relieve the dullness of cooking. Mother felt relief also. She could speak sternly to her children if not to her mother-in-law.

She stopped chopping vegetables long enough to look at both her children. "I am glad I found you both together," she said. "Your father wants the water from one of the fish pools emptied into the other one."

Thu was outraged. "That is not girls' work! Why doesn't Elder Brother do it with Em? A girl is not supposed to do this work."

Mother answered quietly, "Times have changed, or at least this is what you tell me many times. Your father, your grandfather, and your Elder Brother are working in the paddy fields. This is your father's order."

Although he would have liked to have heard more of Grandmother's conversation with Mother, Em went happily. It took great skill to empty one pool into the other. It was a difficult task in every way. Standing opposite each other on the embankments of the pools, each one holding the ends of two long ropes with a tightly woven basket tied to its middle, they had to swing down, fill the basket with water, then swing it up and over so that the basket would empty the water into the other pool. It had to be done with precision, rhythm, and timing. Twisting and turning the body and swinging the heavy, filled basket was hard work. Em remembered it had taken him a long time to learn.

Thu had never done it before, and she was awkward, whereas Em had done it many times and had even taught Sam how to do it. Thu was furious because Em did it so much better. Em knew that since she had carried him on her back she had looked upon him as her baby, someone to help and—if she thought it necessary—to scold. Now he could do this hateful task better than she could do it.

She said, "I know things that you don't know."

Em did not answer. She always had known more than he had.

Thu said, "Old Uncle is disturbed about the stars. He watches them every night, and he grumbles to himself. He is not pleased."

"I know," her brother said. "He told me they did not foretell continued good fortune for our family."

Thu tried swinging the basket again, but she could not do it. "I know something else, too. I know the boy Chi-Bah hopes to marry."

This was something she should not have known and most certainly should not have told. Em looked around. There was no one in hearing distance. "Who is he? Where did you know him? Does he live in the hamlet? Do I know him?"

Thu's face was full of mock horror. "Why, Em," she said in pretended shock, "how could you ask such questions! You know you should not know such things. I'll tell you one thing and no more. He went to school with Anh-Hai and Chi-Bah. They've known each other for years."

"Does our mother know him?"

"If we're going to empty this pool, let's get to work," Thu said.

This was too much for Em. "You don't know how to do

it and I'm wasting time. I'll tell Father to get someone else to help me."

"That's exactly what I wanted," Thu said cheerfully, "and when you get someone to help you empty it, I'll catch more fish than you can."

Em laughed. "You will?"

Both children left for the house, Em to find his father and Thu to go back to the hammock, she hoped. "I have a feeling that any day the Matchmaker will come," she told him. He knew she intended to hear as much as she could.

On the way to the house Em met Sam, who went back with him to empty the pool. "You look tired," Em said. "Perhaps you are too tired to help me."

"After what I've seen, pal, this work will be a peaceful, normal heaven."

"I like it when you come," Em said.

Much later Thu told Em what she had overheard as she crept into the hammock. Her mother and grandmother were still cooking, and they did not notice her. "If such an event should happen," Mother had said, "we will need much money for the feasting." She sighed. "I have very little, although my husband has given me almost all that he has earned. It has taken much to pay for food and the schooling of three children."

"Tomorrow we clean the house," Grandmother said. "The Matchmaker will be looking for something to tell the boy's parents. I know all about that; I've raised and married off a son. The Matchmaker we sent to your house said you seemed to be a good girl, but you were not pretty."

Mother put down her chopping knife. Grandmother had gone too far. "I was very pretty," she said firmly. "Chi-Bah, my Elder Daughter, looks just like I did at her age."

Grandmother laughed. She had been teasing. "Perhaps," she said, "but Thu is more interesting. She talks whether she should or not."

"She is very much like you," Mother said, taking the chopping knife again.

"That's what I said," Grandmother answered with a chuckle. "She is much more interesting than just pretty."

That evening, when they were eating their evening meal, Father asked, "Did you clean the fish pool?"

Thu answered, "Sam helped Em empty the water, but I caught more fish than they did."

Father laughed. He could see his little Thu wading in the muddy bottom of the pool and with her small quick hands catching a basketful of fish. Going to school in Saigon had not changed her. She was still a Vietnamese. He smiled at her.

Old Uncle was silent until the meal was finished. Then he said, not looking at anyone, "A scholar and poet such as I has few intimate friends, unless they be other scholars and poets. But if this be true, they confide in each other. If a man comes here, a man with a beard, which shows he has both age and wisdom, it is apparent that he is a man of good character. He has also been blessed by Heaven with the gift of many children. Em will graze his buffalo tomorrow, and Thu and Sam will help me collect palm fronds for some future use. Let Chi-Bah be her natural and beautiful self. This much I have told you."

Chi-Bah's eyes were downcast, but rose-red showed in her golden cheeks. Everyone but Sam knew what Old Uncle was telling them. Sam asked, "Who is the honorable scholar and poet of good character and many children and why all the preparations?"

No one answered him, and Em could see it was Sam's turn to be embarrassed. Thu said, "I must stay in the house tomorrow. I am going to have a headache."

"The stars say you are as healthy as a young buffalo," Old Uncle replied.

Em was satisfied. Old Uncle would say something to Sam while he and Thu gathered palm fronds, and Thu would tell what she knew. She could not keep anything a secret. For her a secret was something to be told and enjoyed.

Thu told Em that in the course of the day Old Uncle did say to Sam, "It is true, perhaps, what I have heard? That in America young men and women arrange to be married by themselves?" When Sam nodded, Old Uncle said, "I like America. If I were not so old, I would go home with you."

Sam told him, "I'd like to have you, and so would my mother and father."

"Yes, I'd like that. Life is more simple there than here. Here when two people want to marry there are a lot of goings-on. The boy's family send the Matchmaker to find out about the girl and her home and family. Sometimes the girl has never met the boy."

"These two have," Thu told them. "In school. Anh-Hai and Mother know him, too."

Old Uncle was annoyed. He was the one who was supposed to know these things, not this little girl. He said, "I have finished talking about the matter, but first I must know one more thing. Does Chi-Bah like the boy? Will she accept the proposal?"

"You forget, dear Old Uncle," Thu answered, "that Chi-Bah is a proper Vietnamese young lady. She will be very surprised. She will be very reluctant, but why do you think we are getting these palm fronds? We will need them for the wedding, for of course she will accept him. She loves him."

"So much more simple in America. Yes, I think I will visit you when you return to your home there," Old Uncle told Sam.

"Well, I would not call America simple. It has its goings-on too. They are different but just as complex," Sam replied.

At the evening meal no mention was made of the Matchmaker's visit, but all the talk was of the coming engagement and marriage. It was taken for granted that everyone knew that the Matchmaker had come and that he had—in a friendly and informal way—noticed everything about the house and yard, Grandmother and Grandfather, Father and Mother. No one else had been in sight. "Did they like you?" Thu asked.

"Of course," Grandmother answered.

Thu turned to her mother, her face full of mischief. "Do you think that the young man's—whatever his name is—family will like us? Do you think they are a good family?"

Her mother did not answer, but her father said, "They

are like us. When your mother first told me about this, I had them investigated. This is our custom."

The next step would be for Chi-Bah's parents to visit the young man's parents. They did not want to appear overanxious, so they waited a week, while Chi-Bah drooped like a wilted flower and Thu and Em teased her when they could safely do so out of their parents' hearing.

Finally her parents paid the visit, voicing their astonishment at what had happened and expressing their daughter's surprise and reluctance. But they were quick to explain to the parents of Sinh—for that was his name—that she had now overcome the reluctance and was ready for wifehood. "Such a dutiful daughter," Mother told them.

When Em's parents reached home again, they told their waiting family every detail of the visit. Old Uncle said, "And I, in the meantime, have been busy also. I have consulted the best astrologers in Cholon and their horoscopes are good. They tell me that Sinh and Chi-Bah are capable of living together in harmony and goodness."

Sam asked, "What happens next? I must leave and it will be days before I return."

Grandmother replied, "The date has been set for Sinh's parents to meet our little Chi-Bah. Sinh, his parents, and the Matchmaker will come with gifts of fruit and rice wine if they are good people and follow tradition. Chi-Bah will serve the tea and cookies."

"But Mother and Grandmother will make the cookies, I think," Thu told Sam.

"I will make the cookies myself," Chi-Bah said, her eyes flashing.

Sam was surprised. Did Chi-Bah have a quick temper? "They are engaged. Now all they need to do after that is to get married?" he asked.

Mother corrected him. "There are many exchanges of visits between the parents before the engagement date is set," she explained, "and ordinarily two months before the wedding date."

Anh-Hai, who had been present but had taken no part in the conversation, now spoke. "Father, can you spare me from the rice planting so that I may go into Saigon to find out when Sinh and I will be called into the army? It may be that we cannot wait the prescribed two months." This was a problem no one could answer, and it was decided that in the morning Anh-Hai and Sinh should go to Saigon. Em remembered now that for some reason he had felt afraid.

In the morning Sam left too, but he was back by nightfall with a present of two pigs and a quantity of rice wine. "These pigs must be fattened," he told Thu, "and made ready for the wedding feast. I may not be back in time for the wedding," he said to Father, "so if you will permit me, I will leave my wedding gift before I go." Father nodded. Sam took two letters out of his pocket. "I understand," he said, "that wedding gifts are always given in pairs, one to the bride, one to the groom." Again Father nodded. "I have a funny feeling"—Sam seemed embarrassed, but he made himself continue—"that someday these letters may be of use to you. One is to my mother, asking her to treat the little butterfly like a daughter in case she ever comes to America. This letter is for Chi-Bah, and this one"—he gave it to Sinh—"is for you to give to my father if you ever have need to do so."

Both Chi-Bah and Sinh bowed low over Sam's hands as he gave them the letters. "I do not plan to go to America," Sinh said. "Our home is here in the delta of the Mekong. But these letters will be treasures to pass on to our children. We will cherish them." Chi-Bah's eyes were modestly downcast, but she seemed very pleased and touched by the gift. She held her letter with hands that shook.

After Sinh spoke, there was silence in the room, as if a cold wind had blown through the softness of the night, Em now remembered. The boy felt tears sting his eyes, but he did not know why. Grandmother wept openly, but, of course, her age permitted her to show emotion. The others sat silent and erect.

Soon afterward, Sam left them. "Have to be up in the wild blue yonder by dawn," he explained.

"You must get back for our wedding," Chi-Bah said shyly.

"We will be expecting you," Sinh said. "You are part of this family as I am soon to be."

When Sam left the house, Em went with him. "Only for a short distance," Sam told him. "This thing doesn't even stop at night."

"I'll turn back when you tell me to," Em replied.

They walked in silence. There was no need for talk, Em remembered.

"Better turn back now. Remember, when you hear a plane, don't move," Sam had told him. " 'Bye then. I'll try to get back for the wedding, even if it is to be much sooner than they plan. I've a hunch both Anh-Hai and Sinh will be called in a week or two. This thing gets worse by the hour."

"Good-bye, Sam." Em turned back to walk the short distance to the house. He heard no planes. The night was soft and still.

Before Em reached home, he met Old Uncle. "Come walk with me," Old Uncle said. "I am disturbed." This was the second time the old man, usually so confident of the rightness of his knowledge, had talked to Em about what was bothering him.

"Is it about what the stars tell you?" Em asked.

"Yes, by what they tell me. Or perhaps I am getting too old to read them correctly."

Planes flew overhead, stretching their fingers of light over the tree-shadowed path, illuminating anything that moved and could be bombed and made forever still. Old Uncle and Em stood in the shadow of a tomb, as unmoving as the earth and rock, until the planes with their roar of death and their fingers of light became lost in the jungle night.

When there was quiet again, Em asked, "What do the stars tell you, Old Uncle, about the dear ones of our family?"

The old man did not answer.

Em said, "Perhaps it is that you do not want to give me this message?"

"You are my pupil," Old Uncle answered. "For many years you have brought joy to my heart. I have taught you all I know, except the ability to read the stars. You did not have the gift for it."

Em reached out his hand to touch the old one's arm. "I could listen, if that would comfort you."

Old Uncle spoke sadly. "It would not comfort me. For most of our family the message is that they will carry on in the traditional manner of an honorable and ancient family. Then suddenly the message stops."

Em could feel the old man trembling. This was the first time in all his years of living, Em thought, that the stars had failed him, or he had failed them.

"I do not know," Old Uncle said in a troubled voice that shook with the intensity of his emotion. "Maybe the messages stop or perhaps I am getting too old to read them correctly, for they tell me nothing about you. With all your gifts, why could you not have had this important one?"

"I can't read my own," Em confessed, ashamed that he had failed the old one who had given him so much.

Old Uncle said in a tired voice, "Well, I can read mine, but I do not believe what I read. The stars tell me my path will change abruptly and completely, and I will change with it as if someone else walked in my skin. You and I know that is not possible. You and I know that we will not change in our love for each other."

Em asked the question that seemed most important to him. "Do they say nothing about me?"

Uncle said, "Let's walk quickly before another bunch

of those air machines try to find us to kill us." Then he answered Em's question. "You will pay for what you choose to take. You will pay dearly."

"And Sam?" Em asked softly.

The old man was irritated. "I did not see the star that shone on him the night he was born. How can I find it now?"

The planes came again, sending down parachuters with flames that danced like broken stars, down from a troubled sky to a shattered, bomb-scarred land.

"Will peace ever come to our dying land?" Old Uncle asked in a broken voice.

"Yes," Em said with certainty, "Sam says This Thing will pass. Sam says it has to be over soon."

Six

THERE SHOULD HAVE BEEN at least two months of inter-changing visits between Chi-Bah's and Sinh's families before the wedding. But when Anh-Hai and Sinh returned from Saigon, there was great excitement, because both young men were to be called in two weeks. This was unheard of! Grandfather, older by a generation than Anh-Hai's father and the father of Sinh, said, "It is a dangerous act to tamper with and change a tradition, but it is a brave act to change what the Will of Heaven deems must be changed. I feel very strongly that destiny guides us."

The five men listened and nodded. Old Uncle said, "You have spoken wisely, honorable old man. The stars say the wedding will go smoothly. More than that I do not know."

Now that even the date of the wedding would be set within a day or two, Chi-Bah was filled with joy and grief—joy that she was to marry Sinh, and grief that she must leave her family. No one comforted her. There was no time to waste in gentle acts. Besides, she was expected to do her share of the work that must be done.

Em remembered that the first problem had been one of money, or rather, lack of money. There was no time now for Father to go to his friend in Saigon for whom he had always worked. Much money would be needed, for tea and cookies and for fruit and rice wine that now would be served to kin and friends at some event almost every day.

Mother had very little money, but that evening she gave it with pride. Everyone knew she was thrifty. What had been spent had been for a good purpose. But it was such a small amount in its little heap before the Altar of the Ancestors! Em's agonized thought had been, would they have to sell the water buffalo? No one spoke. All eyes were on Mother's money.

Grandmother went down into the tunnel under the house and came back carrying a clay jar almost as large as she was. Em had been surprised. He had thought he knew every twist and turn and dugout in the tunnel, but he had never seen Grandmother's clay jar before. Grandmother dug around inside her pot, prying into it until finally she brought out a handful of money. She placed it with Mother's, saying to Father, "My Son, your father has given me this money through the years to be used in an emergency. This is the first one that you, my Son, have not been able to manage. Your father and I are honored to give the money to you."

Father bowed before the Altar of the Ancestors, and then, turning, he bowed over Grandmother's hands. The old lady began to cry. Thu was the first to hug and pat her shaking shoulders.

Father bowed over Mother's hands, saying, his voice deep with emotion and affection, "My Own, you have given my parents, me, and our children every hour of your life. Even your years in Saigon, which I knew you hated, but which I thought would be of benefit to the three I sent with you." Em had never heard his father call his mother "My Own," before, although he had heard young husbands calling their young wives by that endearment. He had never known his father to speak with such love and affection. Now he saw him not only as a father, wise and firm in his decisions, but also as a man, loving and tender.

The formal visits kept on day after day. First the groom, his family, and his friends paraded across the rice paddy with trays of gifts, fruit, and rice wine. The following day it was the bride's family with trays of tea and cookies.

After several more formal visits and formal conversations between both sets of parents, it was considered that a wedding would be forthcoming. "I never heard Chi-Bah say she was willing to marry Sinh," Em had told Thu. "When did all this happen?"

Thu laughed. "I did not hear it either, but this I know. If our Elder Sister had *not* wanted to marry Sinh, she would have told our parents and the getting-to-know-each-other visits would have ended long ago."

Em looked at his sister with admiration. "Girls know a lot of things that boys don't know," he told her, adding quickly, "Not important things, of course, being girls—how could they?" Then, softening what he thought had been too harsh, he said, "But interesting things I like to hear."

Thu did not answer. Furious at being just a girl and knowing nothing important, she was also flattered that what she knew was considered interesting. There was nothing she could think of in answer. Em looked at her in surprise. Thu's silence was something to think about.

The next day Sam came back just for the day, to help build a new pavilion of palm fronds and branches so that all the kin and guests of both families could be seated for the engagement and wedding feasts. The houses had to be cleaned and decorated with branches and flowers and great piles of fruit in the corners of the rooms. This had been Anh-Hai's and Em's work, and of course Sam had helped them. Em remembered that the women and girls had cooked all day. Sam must have been too shy to ask Grandmother for a bite of this and that in front of the crowd of teasing girls and women, and he became hungry and irritable.

Em knew that Sam had to leave the day before the engagement feast and that he was not unhappy that he had to go. This time Sam was walking back to camp—having neither jeep nor motorcycle—so Em walked part of the way with him. Suddenly Sam said to Em, "Why can't they just get engaged by saying yes when there's no one around to hear them? This parading across the paddy fields day after day isn't necessary! And with all those fancy clothes and the colored parasols waving over their heads."

Em was shocked and deeply offended, but he could see that Sam, too, was appalled at what he had said. Quickly Sam tried to make amends by joking. "Imagine if I were marrying a Vietnamese girl in her hamlet. Just picture me, buddy, trying to walk alongside all those doll-like creatures with their grace and charm. I'm twice as tall as they are and ten times as awkward." Sam looked at Em out of the corner of his eye.

Em pictured Sam in a brightly flowered robe and a long sash, trying to carry a tray of rice wine and fruit in one hand and balance a bright-colored parasol in the other as he strode along with the line of tiny, graceful, formal Vietnamese. Em usually could hide his emotions, but this was too much. In a moment he burst into laughter, and Sam joined him. When Em could control his mirth, he said shyly, "We were walking a shaky bridge in our friendship. Where are we now?"

Sam was still laughing. "We fell off that shaky bridge and we are in the middle of the river."

"Swimming?" Em asked in a low voice.

"You bet we're swimming, and we can make both sides of the bank any time we want to," Sam answered him and then was serious. "That means, Em, that from now on you and I are friends. We do not need to worry if we are American or Vietnamese. Just friends, ready to give and take."

Em's smile was radiant. "What do you suppose made

us friends? You were sitting there and I was watching you and wishing I could talk to you. Remember?"

Sam nodded. "I remember very well. I was needing someone to talk to."

"But you did not know I was there."

"No," Sam admitted, "but maybe I did. I don't really know how friendships begin. They just happen."

After a pause Em said, "There is something that has been bothering me. What was the paper you were reading so carefully? Was it a list of your ancestors?"

Sam laughed. "No. It was a letter from my girl."

"Your girl! Do you have an Elder Daughter, Sam?" Em asked.

Sam did not laugh this time. His answer was serious and it seemed to Em to be full of pain. "No Elder Daughter, Em. I'm not married. It was from the girl I want to marry."

"Won't the Matchmaker arrange for the wedding? Will your girl accept you? Do you have the bride's price?"

"We don't have those things in America," Sam explained. "The trouble is, she's tired of waiting for me to come home from Vietnam. I want to go home. No one knows how much I want to go home, but something keeps me here. I want Americans to know what is really happening here. I love America. I want my countrymen to know what they're doing to the land and the people half a world away from our peaceful shores." Sam said good-bye hurriedly as if, Em thought, he were afraid of unleashing his own bitterness.

Now Em laughed, thinking of the long day that had followed filled with polite conversation and grave anxiety by both families. Sinh hoped what they had to offer was enough, but not more than the bride was worth. Chi-Bah's parents had wanted what their child was worth. At last both families were satisfied. Chi-Bah's price had been high in jewelry, in woven cloth, and a huge amount of money. Both mothers smiled happily at each other, one thinking, My beautiful daughter has great value; the other, How fortunate, my son can have a valuable wife.

"A new line," Grandfather said, "strong and good."

Father was satisfied. No American soldier could marry Elder Daughter now. The line would be kept pure. "At first," Father confided to Grandfather, "I was afraid she might have the foolish desire to marry Sam."

Grandfather laughed. "Sam is an American. Nothing else but an American would tempt him."

Em knew Father was a little upset over Grandfather's statement. Sam's not being tempted by Chi-Bah was different from Chi-Bah's not being interested. "Chi-Bah," Grandfather said, "is very determined for a girl. I'm glad we did not need to order her not to fall in love with Sam."

Father saw the wisdom in this remark. "You are right, respected Father," he said, and both men smiled. It was good to live in harmony.

The days after were more work-filled than the ones before the engagement party. A new, much larger pavilion had to be built because kin and guests of both families would come from as far distant as Cholon and Saigon and villages in between. The man for whom Father had worked in Saigon when he needed money was coming with his wife, his married son and daughter-in-law. The daughter-in-law was a Vietnamese, and his son had been trained in the United States and was now a major in the Vietnamese Army. Everyone was pleased that they were coming—Mother, because she knew the family and liked them; Grandmother, because a major in the army would eat her cooking and like it, also; Father, because he had a plan. He thought it would work.

Thu was feeling very neglected now that all the attention was being given to Elder Sister, although lately she and Em had become friends. Suddenly she had not been Em's boss, and just as suddenly she had not wanted to be. Being sister and brother had been enough—until the Matchmaker had come asking for Chi-Bah. "Will a Matchmaker ever come for me?" Thu asked Em. "I know I'll never bring as high a bride price, but I will be more fun." Then without waiting for a reply, she continued, "Anh-Hai and Chi-Bah are more serious, but you and I will always live in this hamlet and from dawn to dark we will walk with happiness."

Em laughingly agreed. "Old Uncle said I brought joy to his heart, and Grandmother insists I make laughter live in this house."

"And now that I've come home to stay, there will be twice as much joy and laughter," Thu said. "Who cares if the Matchmaker never comes for me!"

"I wish Sam were here. We three could have fun," Em replied.

"Yes, I like Sam too. He is almost like a brother," Thu answered wistfully.

At last the wedding day had come, and as Old Uncle said, the stars had predicted it would be a bright, still day—warm, but not breathtakingly hot. Even the night before the wedding day had been bright with stars and a full golden moon, and what was almost frighteningly surprising, not a single plane had filled the night with terror. It was a night to remember.

The festivities began at Sinh's house. All the guests brought gifts of money to help pay the bride's price, which they suspected was enormous. "Has she not come from a proud and ancient family?" they whispered behind their fans. "Has she not been educated in the French school in Saigon and has learned how to be a secretary in the American school there?" they said, eyeing the growing mound of gift money on the table before the Ancestral Altar. "Besides, her mother has trained her in the duties of a Vietnamese wife and mother," Sinh's mother told no one in particular, but everyone heard.

At last the wedding was over. Chi-Bah had taken off her rented red robe and circular hat and had dressed in her working clothes. She and Sinh went among the guests, serving them food and seeing that they had everything they wanted, Chi-Bah among the women and Sinh among the men. Now even this had been finished. The guests had walked homeward across the paddy fields. Sinh and Chi-Bah, who had not spoken to each other or eaten, now had gone to the pavilion to eat what was left of the feast.

The wedding was over. The guests had gone and the house was being restored to order. The pavilion had been taken down and the logs piled behind the house to be used for some other occasion. All the bowls and cups and glasses that had been borrowed from the neighbors were washed and returned. There was an empty feeling in the house and in the hearts of the family. Father and Mother invited the major and his wife to stay after the departure of the other guests.

The major and Father and Mother talked together. Their talk was serious and quiet. Finally Anh-Hai and Sinh were called into the conference. At last, when all the helpers had gone to their homes and only the family was left, Father told Em to go for Sinh's father and mother. Father told them to be seated on their mats grouped around the Altar of the Ancestors.

Father said to his listening family, "This may be the last time all of us will be together. As you know, the war worsens. The VC are everywhere; they will capture and kill all of us who have been friendly with the Americans. I have known this for a long time. We who love our government must help in any way we can. I have known the major since he was a small boy and watched me fix and drive his father's cars. He now wants me to come to Saigon to be his military chauffeur. I will work as a civilian as I am too old for the army, and I will live in a part of the palace that has been set aside for civilian employees of the military. Anh-Hai and Sinh will be regular soldiers, and Chi-Bah will go with her husband and live in a barracks that is for the soldiers who are married, but she will also have an active part in the war. She will be the major's secretary." This was Father's plan—to keep them together as much as possible.

Em remembered that there was a complete silence in the room; only the night insects chirped their vesper songs.

72

Finally Chi-Bah spoke. "Father—" Then she corrected herself. Her husband was the one she obeyed now. "My Husband—" She stopped in embarrassment. This was the first time she had addressed him as "Husband." "My Own"—she used the accepted Vietnamese term—"when do we go? When do we leave our loved ones?"

It was the major who answered. "Now. Within an hour's time. We will be expected to answer this evening's roll call."

"Now?" Chi-Bah asked faintly. "Now? Not one more day in my loved home?"

"No," the major said.

Em sat unmoving. He had known this was coming, but now that it had come, he did not know what to do.

At last Mother spoke. "What will you need to take?"

"They will be issued uniforms and the necessary clothing," the major said. "Chi-Bah must travel light. It is usual for wives to accompany their husbands when they go from place to place."

"I will take my husband's gifts of necklaces and earrings and Sam's letters," Chi-Bah said. "Should I take your letter that Sam wrote to his father for you, My Own?"

Sinh said, "No," at first. Then he said, "Yes. You take them both. They will be safer with you, and we will never be separated. I promise you."

Chi-Bah smiled at him. "We will be together. I promise too."

Old Uncle said, "Do not defy the stars. They are the holders of your destiny."

"Then what do they tell us?" Grandmother asked.

But as usual Old Uncle did not answer her. He had not listened to what she said.

There were a few minutes of silence. Em felt a need to comfort all of them, but he did not know what to do or say. Silently he went to stand beside his mother, but she seemed not to feel his nearness. Then Mother did an unusual, an unexpected, an unheard-of thing. She walked into Father's outstretched arms and put her head on his shoulder. They did not speak, but stood silently together, Father holding her tenderly and Mother looking tired and defeated. Em and his family looked at them unbelievingly. Mother had always been so strong and brave, Father so quietly calm. At last the major touched Father's arm. It was time to go. Even then they did not speak. Their love was silent and strong. It would endure forever.

Within an hour they were gone, Father driving the major's car. Em stood with Mother in the darkening night, looking until they disappeared: Father; Anh-Hai, firstborn son; Chi-Bah, Elder Daughter; and the boy, Sinh, not yet twenty-one. No one was left but the very old, the two young children, and Mother to transplant the rice and work the paddy fields. How much could they plant? Would there be enough harvest to feed them? they wondered.

A plane flew overhead. Now the night's bombing had started with the threat of death shadowing their thoughts. Would their light point out the major's car and bring death to the dear ones it held? Em wondered. "Something tells me we will not meet again," Mother murmured, forgetting Em was at her side. "Maybe some will be spared,

74

but not all. Some will be missing. My husband, my first-born, my Elder Daughter," and each word showed deeper pain. She braced herself against the palm-frond wall. "I am not the only one," she said to Em. "This very second there are a thousand mothers saying good-bye to their dear ones forever, Americans as well as our own people. Why?" she asked the blinking stars. "Why is there savage war?" Her only answer was a bomb going off quite near. "Never an answer to the why of war," she said clearly, defying destiny—if that was what it was—and took Em's hand and went into the house.

Together they looked at the sleeping family. "As always they are my responsibility," she said to Em, "greater now, since I stand between them and the war that threatens us from enemy and friend alike, and with no husband within calling distance to share my fear for our safety. But I have you, Em—I am not completely alone." Grandmother and Thu were curled up together, so alike, so merry and talkative and mischief-filled and underneath so lost and afraid. Grandfather prayed before the Altar of the Ancestors. Old Uncle sat outside, gazing at the stars. He had an inner strength; confused and questioning as it had become, he still felt it strong enough to ask for help, strong enough to look for some sign that could be an answer.

Mother stood at the entrance of her darkened house, looking at the night flares dancing downward upon the land. What did she have, she wondered, except love for her family and pity for people who let hate and greed and stubbornness tear them to shreds, defile the land, and wash life and beauty and hope from the face of the earth?

PART 2 | Seven

AFTER THE ACTIVITY of the wedding and the agony of the departing of the family, time seemed to drag. The house and yard that had been so full of laughing people now seemed empty and too quiet. The wedding had made everyone forget the war for a time, but now it was as if it had never been, or as if it had taken place a long time ago, when formality and tradition were the way of life. Now the way of life was lying in the dirt of the road or the mud of a footpath as giant bombers swept the sky.

The days and the nights passed slowly but not in idleness. The thatch on the house roof had to be repaired. Reeds and palm fronds had to be gathered and made ready for weaving new seat mats for the floor before the

Altar of the Ancestors, and for the woven partitions of the rooms and the outside walls.

There were other daily chores—mending the breaks in the canals caused by the night-dropping bombs before the whole embankment crumbled under the force of the water; hauling away the bomb-felled trees that blocked the spur roads and footpaths and chopping them into wood for the fires of the cold-wind months and the monsoon rains. Broken and burned bodies had to be carried to the over-filled, understaffed hospitals and the dead buried in hastily dug trenches. There were no tombs built so that the spirits released from the dead bodies might have an eternal resting place. When peace came there would be time for building tombs, but there was no time for such things now. Now was for trying to keep the living alive.

The days were also filled with the small ordinary tasks—sharpening a plow, mending fish baskets. Sometimes, Em thought, there seemed to be as many kinds of fish baskets as there were fish to trap in them. Em took the buffalo to rest and stand, contented, in the water of the river and the canals, or out to graze in the early morning and to rest in his clean straw shelter during the day's heavy heat. The days were full of small, necessary tasks and the nights full of the roar of the planes, threatening all life and dropping the implements of death at random.

This was the last of the dry season, the lull before the exhausting activity of rice planting. Rice planting must be planned in each small detail. Everything happened in relationship to what had happened the day—almost the hour—before. Long before actual planting there were questions to be asked and correctly answered. How much rice would the family need from this year's harvest to the next one? There was no thought now of surplus rice to sell or of an opportunity to buy. Transportation was too risky; the roads were too hazardous to carry it on one's back. How much of their land could they plant, cultivate, and harvest—three old people, two children, and a mother, strong and courageous but very tired? They could not even attempt it without their young, strong buffalo. A few wealthy families had a team or two, but most families, like Em's, had only one. They knew without talking about it that they could plant only enough to feed themselves. It had never happened before that they had fields that were unplanted, but it would happen this year.

"Can we rent the land we cannot use?" Old Uncle asked.

Grandfather did not think it possible. "All our problems are the same. We have not enough people to work the land," he said sadly. "There will be more people to eat the rice at harvest than there will be to plant and tend it."

Mother said cheerfully, "We will do all we can. The Book of Heaven could not tell us to do more than that."

The others nodded in agreement.

Em's family was not one of the wealthy ones in the hamlet. Their land holding was small, but for certain parts of the planting they had always hired help. There had always been poor young people and needy old ones who, having no land of their own, worked for their more fortunate neighbors. This year Em's family had money. Father and Anh-Hai sent home their earnings, and Chi-Bah would help if it was needed. But there were no laborers to be hired. The strong young men were at war or dead or captured as prisoners of war. The old ones were fewer in number. The war years had taken them also. But the rice had to be planted.

Grandfather planned carefully. The fields near the canals could be irrigated in the old way that Grandfather had used when he was young. When a field was to be flooded with water, a small opening was dug in its embankment and the water flowed in. When this field was flooded, the opening was plugged and a new opening was dug in another embankment and another field was irrigated. When all the fields had a suffficient amount of water, the openings were closed and the canal water flowed its natural course.

The fields at a greater distance from the canal could be irrigated with the foot-paddle waterwheel. The foot-paddle waterwheel was very simple and in Grandfather's thinking very efficient—much better, he thought, than the gasoline pump his son had rented these past few years. Grandfather said to Old Uncle, "While my son is winning the war driving the major around, I will be growing rice in the way it has been grown for thousands of years, the way it should be grown." Grandfather got out the old waterwheel and looked it over. "Good as new and simple to operate," he told Old Uncle.

Old Uncle looked it over. "Same one," he said. Wooden paddles were set in a hub making the hub go clockwise. Other wooden paddles were attached to each side to be paddled by the operator who leaned on a bar.

"The young one," Grandfather said, "will be delighted with it."

Old Uncle laughed. "I remember one year I had to operate this same waterwheel," he said. "That was the year I decided to be a scholar."

Remembering it now, Em thought, at first he *had* been delighted. Being able to push water forward had been fun for a while, but he could feel the pain in his legs as he paddled and paddled the heavy water. He wondered if Old Uncle had been joking or if that was really the reason for his becoming a scholar.

"What about fertilizer?" Old Uncle asked.

Everyone was surprised at his question. Always before Old Uncle had been interested only in words and in ideas. Mother smiled lovingly at him. She was touched by his concern for such workaday matters. Grandmother chuckled. She was pleased. She had been his older sister who had cared for him before he became a poet and a scholar.

To Grandfather, however, it was an ordinary question. "What can be more important than fertilizer to a rice field?" he asked, looking at Grandmother. Grandmother chuckled again. She had her own secret thoughts. Em did not enter into the conversation, but he listened, interested in everything that was said.

Grandfather, also, had thought about it, but he had solved the problem. To buy the commercial fertilizer that the young farmers were using they would need to go to Cholon. Three old people could never make it there and back. Before the bridge had been bombed, there had been a bus that went, if and when there were people wanting to go somewhere, but both the bridge and the bus had been destroyed. Mother and the children could go and probably get home again, but it was better not to try it, Grandfather thought. He wanted them safe at home.

"That fertilization is a problem," he said. "Yes, that's a problem." He let them worry a bit. Then he said, slapping his withered old hand against his shaking legs, "We'll make our own. The way I used to make it, and I was considered the best rice-growing farmer in the delta. We will use the ash I saved when we burned the rice stalks last harvest and add to it the rich compost of leaves and plants and buffalo chips I've been preparing. Looked at it yesterday. It's ripe for using."

Em remembered how he hated the horrible-smelling stuff and would much rather have used what his father bought, but he said nothing. Grandfather was in charge. He was the Authority. One yielded to Authority.

The weeks before planting time, Em remembered now, had been almost unbearable. It seemed to him that the dry season had never been so dry. The ground was parched and cracked, the air was so still, and the yellow heat of the long day's sun smothered him with exhaustion. The heat pressed down from the sky and thrust itself up from the earth, and the hours moved slowly through the days and the nights. So hot. So dry. So long. Would the rains never come? Old Uncle looked at the stars and was satisfied. Em was restless. Besides, he missed his father and brother and sister. Missing them seemed to add to the unbearable heat. Sam had not come for a long time. Had he gone to America? Em wondered. He feared he had, but somehow he knew Sam was still with his Vietnamese people. Why did he like them? Em wondered. Deep within his heart Em thought Sam really did not *like* them but felt a bond, a sort of brotherhood with them. "Like he feels for me," Em confided to his buffalo. Like everything else, it added to the confusion of his days.

At last one night the water buffalo moved restlessly. Em, who had been sleeping beside his buffalo every night since his father had gone, was instantly awake. "I feel it too," he said softly to the great creature standing beside him. The boy felt a kind of vibration against his sweat-dried skin, a smell of dampness in the still, hot air, a murmur swelling into a sound as it came. It was the southwest wind; he knew it was the monsoon wind bringing the rain. Bringing the chilling cold, too, he remembered, but a relief from the hot, dry season.

The dry season was ended. The rain had come, and now the fields and the seedbed could be made ready for the planting of the rice. The rain came at first in a gentle patter, but by dawn it was a steady pouring of rain upon the thirsty land. Everyone was rejoicing.

They ran outside with a feeling of the joy of rain against their sun-blackened bodies. Nerves that had been taut were now free as the wind. "The rains have come!" they shouted. "The rains have come!"

They watched the water in the fields, at first wetting the land, but gradually soaking it, saturating it, and making the mud that was needed so much for the rice seedlings.

After the joy of the first rain came the anxiety natural to a people whose lives were directed by the Book of Heaven. What was to be would be. They accepted this. They were reconciled to it, but they worried. Would the Heaven-sent rain stop too soon for the rice to get its beginning growth? Would it rain too much so that the new roots rotted? In their eagerness to get started, would they choose the right planting date? Would the Will of Heaven cause some delay that would damage the crop?

Old Uncle consulted the stars and for the first time in many months rejoiced in what they foretold. It would rain enough. It would stop soon enough. He and the other Venerables of the hamlet consulted the calendar for the right date for planting and from that date worked backward to the time when the preparation of the seedbeds and the fields should be started. The few families who had a team of buffalo could work them and rest them and work them again for an eight-hour day. The men's endurance did not count—it was the strength of the buffalo that must always be considered. All the one-buffalo families worked their animals five hours a day from six in the morning until eleven. Then the animals grazed and rested until the next morning.

Em, thinking backward, remembered he had said to his grandmother, not looking at his grandfather, "I know my buffalo very well. I know what he likes, and what he likes I like to give him." Em stopped talking, hoping his grandfather would ask what it was that his buffalo liked, but no one asked him anything. If he had something that he thought must be said, he could say it, but of his own accord. No one was going to help him. After waiting awhile he continued. "My buffalo likes to get up at five o'clock. If we went to work at five o'clock instead of six, we could rest an hour halfway and still finish what needs to be done by eleven o'clock."

No one answered him. Em turned to look at his grandfather. "I don't want my buffalo to work for five long hours without a rest."

Grandfather, looking at Em, could see challenge in his determination to preserve his buffalo.

Em remembered this now. He remembered his grandfather looking at him for, it seemed, a long, long time. He was frightened, but he did not flinch. No one understood, he thought, how much he loved his buffalo. He loved his little grandmother very much, but his buffalo and Sam were his companions. He would do anything for them, he thought as he looked at his grandfather's stern and unyielding face. If no one helped him, he would stand alone.

Finally the grandfather spoke. "Grandson." He had never called him anything but "young one" before. "Grandson, I think you are right. Getting up at five o'clock will be good for you and your animal. But remember"—now the old man spoke sternly—"five o'clock is five o'clock and not five minutes after five."

"I will never be late," Em had said, and now he remembered that he never had been, although at times five o'clock had seemed to be the middle of the night.

Guiding a buffalo drawing a heavy plow, keeping the rows straight through the knee-deep mud of the rice field, is difficult work. It was a man's work, not a boy's, but Em and his buffalo seemed to be so much a part of each other that each gave the other strength.

Plowing was difficult, but harrowing was harder. The plow had weight and a heavy steel blade, but the harrow had only a rake. Someone had to stand on the rake to weigh it down as Em guided the buffalo drawing the harrow through the mud. Grandfather tried, but he was too old and became dizzy, falling, under their frightened gaze, in the mud beside the moving rake. Grandmother tried and loved it, but she was so light the rake touched only the surface of the mud. That morning as they were trying to decide if Mother and Thu could hang on together, Sam came walking quickly down the path. Em cried, "Sam! You always come when we need you."

"I try," Sam said, laughing. Then he spoke seriously. "Can you stop work for a bit? I have something for the little butterfly."

The family crowded around him, the buffalo, as always, standing patient and still. What Sam carried so tenderly was a wet pasteboard box without even a cover.

"A present for me?" Thu wanted to know. "A present from America?" Sam shook his head. He was more serious than they had ever seen him. "No, Little Butterfly, not from America and not a present." He stopped talking to make certain that Thu understood that this was not a game he was playing with her. "This is not a present," he repeated. "It is a responsibility. Are you old enough to take it?"

"I'm thirteen," Thu replied with dignity. "Em will tell you I always do my share." Thu was silent, and then she added in a voice so low that it almost could not be heard and yet so from the heart that it could be heard by everyone, "Sam, I can try."

"That's my little butterfly," Sam said, kneeling in the mud and putting the small, wet box he was carrying down gently beside him.

Now, as he remembered that moment, Em bent farther over the table, putting his head on his tablet. He closed his eyes, but he could still see what was in the box. As long as he lived he would see it. When anyone, a stranger passing him on the street, carried a box, Em could see in it what he had seen in this one. He could hear again what his grandfather had said to him that day in the orphanage, "Let the boy vomit. It will relieve the pain in his belly. . . ." A pain in the belly was nothing, the boy had thought, looking into the box.

He could not vomit. He could only look, and the pain was in his eyes, his head, his stomach, his heart—the whole of him—and yet he could not stop looking. In the box was a baby—at least it looked like a baby—with nothing but a dirty rag around it. It was so thin that only a kind of skin held its bones together. But it was alive. Its eyes were alive—deep, dark pools of bleakness, looking at nothing, seeing nothing, telling nothing but that a thin thread of life was somewhere within the bundle of bones.

Thu was the first one to speak. "A baby, a beautiful, dear little baby, for me, Sam?" Grandmother made a soft crooning sound, holding out her withered, shaking arms to gather the baby into them, but Thu acted first. She lifted the baby tenderly to cradle it to her heart. "Little dear," she whispered. "Little dear, you are home. Sam found you."

Sam began to cry, tears streaming down his face. "I almost stepped on it—up the road a bit. I would have gone back to the military hospital with it. It's so small, but I thought they could find a crack someplace to put it. I almost started back, and then I thought of the little butterfly and how she would give it love as well as care. Did I do right, *Me*?" This was the first time he had ever called Mother by the Vietnamese word *Me*.

Em had looked at him in astonishment. He was truly one of the family now. He had called their mother *Me*. Then they all looked with greater astonishment at their mother. She was crying, not just with tears, but with sobs that seemed to tear her apart. None of them had ever seen their mother cry before. She had always been so ready to ease their hurts; they had never thought that she herself had need for tears. "It's the war," she sobbed. "I cannot stand the killing of people, all people, our enemies as well as our relatives and friends. I cannot stand the eternal noise as the planes fly above us. And now this poor little bag of bones that a mother abandoned to starve."

"Maybe she was killed," Sam said awkwardly, wiping his eyes.

"Killed?" Mother cried. "Killed? Even in death a mother would have held her child to shelter it. War is evil. It makes all it touches evil."

As quickly as Mother had cried out, she became silent. In a moment she spoke in almost her normal voice. "Grandmother and Thu, take the small one to the house.

You will know what to do with it. I will do your work here."

"I will do their work, *Me*," Sam said.

"How long can you stay?" Grandfather asked.

"As long as you need me," Sam answered. "The Americans can miss reading about body counts for a while. I'm almost written dry, anyway. I write the same things over and over. Body counts! Body counts! What does it mean?"

"It means the number of people who are dead," Thu said, not knowing they understood. "I can't see how they can count so many."

"Stand on the rake, Sam," Grandfather said, as if Thu had not spoken, "to weigh it down. The buffalo will draw it through the mud while the young one guides it."

"That's a man's job," Sam objected. "Let Em stand on the rake. I'll do the wading through the mud."

Everyone laughed. "You couldn't guide the buffalo," they told him.

"The young one is the only boy in the hamlet who can do it," Grandmother added. "There's something between the boy and the buffalo, as if they were brothers. If it is the Will of Heaven, may they never be parted."

Old Uncle said nothing.

The pattern of preparing the seedbed and the fields did not change—plow-harrow-plow-harrow, repeat six times with two or three days in between to air the earth. "Let it rest," they said. "The ground must be tilled," they said, "finely tilled."

The rice seeds had been soaked in water for several days and then put in a basket which was kept damp for the seeds to germinate. Now the anxious questions were, "Are the rice seeds sprouting?" "Are they growing as rapidly as they should?" "Will they have grown too tall before we have the seedbeds ready?"

But always with these questions of anxiety there were exclamations of joy about the new baby. There had been many long discussions about what they would name the baby. Thu had only one suggestion, and she held firmly to it and finally won. She wanted the baby to be Number Two Sam, which finally became Sami-two. As the days went by, someone would say in breathless wonder, "Sami-two's eyes moved. They follow Thu. Sami-two recognizes Thu." "Her eyes light up when she sees her." "Sami-two moved a hand—not both hands, just one." "Sami-two eats. She gobbles her food."

As strength came to Sami-two and flesh began to cover the naked bones, other problems developed. She began to cry. Em remembered saying, "She cries like an old woman," and his grandfather answering, "Why shouldn't she cry like an old woman? Her heart already has known the bitterness of age." The crying spells came mostly at night when the baby screamed and screamed and stiffened her thin little body. Hour after hour Thu rocked her and sang old Vietnamese songs to her, and gradually the spells became less frequent and of shorter duration.

Sam worried about the extra burden he had put upon the family. "I should have taken her to the hospital, *Me*, but they have time only to give the children food and water, and I thought this little baby needed the tender love the little butterfly would give her."

"You were right to bring her here," Mother answered. "She needs love as well as care, and we have plenty of that to give her."

Grandfather was more stern with his answer. "Her crying is a good sign. It shows she has at least some mentality. She is remembering, even though she does not know what it is she remembers. Think of those babies lying cot by cot in the hospital," he went on. "Perhaps their bodies may be somewhat mended, but I can't forget the look in their eyes. I wish I knew why we have war—war—war. War has been our history. I am not only tired for myself—I am tired for my race, for all men."

The planting must go on. The sproutings were of the right height. The sprouting seeds were now scattered over the muddy surface of the seedbeds. No more water was allowed in the seedbeds. The seeds must be given time to settle firmly in the mud.

Again the men consulted the calendar for the right time to transplant the sprouting seedlets to the paddy fields that were ready to receive them. Now the most backbreaking work of all began. One man collected a handful of seedlings. If he was experienced, his handful could contain about thirty of the delicate plants. He slapped the paddy dirt from them by hitting them against his leg. In this too he had to have experience. Too hard a slap might break the tender plants. Then he tied each bundle with a cord twisted from palm fronds. These bundles were collected and carried in bamboo baskets, tied to the ends of their shoulder poles.

The family was able to hire three boys to help in this work, so Sam, Old Uncle, Em, and the three boys took the bundles from Grandfather and planted them, making a long line in a straight row across the field. Grandfather insisted they sing as they worked to keep the rhythm of planting and relieve the backbreaking torture. But only Grandfather and Old Uncle knew the songs that had been sung in the old days when men worked with their hands and sang to keep their bodies moving in rhythm as each man stopped to plant four seedlings, only four, in the mud of the paddy. Since only two of the men knew these songs and the others did not, the experience ended in laughter and jokes about singing as a healing for back-aches. Grandfather did not join in the joking or the laughter. He said, "What has been done many thousand years by many thousands of people should continue. I don't know much about such things, but I think even plants need the touch of the heart. It's a bond binding their needs together."

The men listened in respectful silence, not that they believed what he said, but in reverence for his age. Em had expected Old Uncle to say something, but he too was silent. The boy wondered why Old Uncle had not taught him the songs of the people instead of the ancient poems and the history, long gone by. But perhaps the rice responded to laughter rather than memorized melodies. He thought about it for a long time and forgot that his back ached from the constant twisting to get the four seedlings and the bending down to plant their roots safely in the mud.

The weather held well, and after a time the rice was

planted. There were a few weeks of anxiety for fear the rice would not grow into healthy plants or the weather would change or a rice disease would spread among the paddies. Weeds were almost no problem, and besides, weeding was women's work. There was no cause for worry: the women would work as much as needed, and whenever it was necessary.

As far as the rice crop was concerned, Old Uncle was satisfied. There were no ill omens among the stars—not for the rice. As for the family members, Old Uncle became angry when they asked him questions. Mother told her children, "What is to be must be. Accept what must be accepted," and all but Old Uncle lived from hour to hour with neither hope nor despair. They called it destiny.

Eight

THE WAR CONTINUED. The body count, the uncounted
burned and crippled, and the thousands of orphaned
and abandoned children, the burned hamlets, the destroyed roads and waterways 'grew steadily in tragic
number, but the pattern of life of the people who remained in the deltas was little changed. They revered
their dead, they gave good example to their children, and
they accepted the Will of Heaven. Most years their rice
crop had thrived.

The delta had been where it now was since the beginning of time, or so the people thought, and the different
roaming bands, the wandering tribes, and—in later centuries—the settled nations had poured over it like the

tides of the sea—moving in, spreading out, receding. Then new waves of people moving in, spreading out, receding, century after century, but both the land and the growing of rice remained, and little was changed.

After the first weeks of transplanting the rice all seemed well with its natural development, and from then until September, when the fields drooped with their heavy-laden stacks of golden grain and the air was sweet with the fragrance of ripened rice, the people returned to the ordinary daily tasks.

Em spent his days with his buffalo, finding shaded spots for it to graze in the morning hours, finding deep water holes where it could enjoy quiet coolness, and daily bringing clean, dry straw to its shelter. Em had his buffalo, and he had Sam.

Sam did not come to the hamlet as often any more. He seemed more quiet, more serious. He never played ball with the boys, but he almost always had candy to give them. "Where's your bubble gum?" the little boys would ask. "Why no more bubble gum?" and Sam would look at Em, and they would laugh. The boys would say in Vietnamese, "Why does he not have bubble gum, and why does he laugh about it? It isn't good to laugh about what you don't have and others want." But they liked Sam. He treated them as equals and friends. They liked that. Sam always had a line of boys, little and half-grown, tagging after him, but he had time for Em, too, when he visited the hamlet, and they had long talks, and Old Uncle joined them when he was not too busy with the stars.

"Why don't you come to the hamlet as often as you

used to? Are you getting tired of us?" Thu asked one day.

"No, Little Butterfly, but I am getting tired of war and what I have to write about it. Coming to the hamlet is like coming home."

"For us too, my Son," Mother told him, and Em saw Sam turn away before she could see the tears in his eyes.

The family spent the long hours together, jesting and laughing, playing games and singing. Seemingly they were happy and contented, but in each heart there was a secret hurt, and the night hours were heavy with the pain of their fears, the dread of knowing that what was to be would be, and the worry for the ones who were not with them.

Em knew how Grandfather must feel. He missed his son, his firstborn, the one who was to carry on the family name. Until the day Em's father had gone to war, Grandfather had been satisfied and thought that he had well earned the contentment of old age. He had raised his son by good example, and his son had rewarded him a hundredfold. The son had a good wife, two fine sons, and also two daughters, and while, of course, the girls were not as important as the sons, they were pretty little things, and one of them had already brought a handsome bride price and was now the wife of a son of good family from a neighboring hamlet. But now Em could see that Grandfather's days of contentment and meditation were over. All the decisions had again been placed upon his shoulders, and he seemed old and tired and shared with the rest of the family the constant fear that death or torture might come to his son or elder grandson and, if the war lasted long enough, even to the young one. If this happened, his family would end. The name and all it stood for would be gone. The old man prayed that this would not be written in the Book of Heaven. Grandfather thought he had obeyed the Laws of Heaven. Had he failed? Where had he failed? How had he failed? He asked for spiritual enlightenment.

Em could tell that Mother missed her husband and children. She feared for their lives, for their welfare, for their morals. She prayed by the Altar of the Ancestors and by the smaller Altar for the Household Spirit. "I will accept what must be accepted," she prayed, "but if I have angered you, how may I atone? I want my husband and my children safe with me. What can I do to mend my mistakes?"

Old Uncle was clearly outraged. He hated the stars for what they told him, and he feared his hate for the vengeance the stars might pour down on his family. He muttered to himself bitterly, "I am a scholar, but also I am a man who hates."

Em feared that Sam would forget to come. He knew with his mind that Sam came as often as he could and stayed as long as he thought he should, but each time Sam left, the boy feared he would forget to come back. Sam would go to America, as he was always saying he wanted to go home, although he could not go. So Em stayed on the fringes of the swamp and the edges of the jungle and played his flute and sang the songs Old Uncle had taught him. He worried but did not fear.

All the family loved Sami-two. The first time she laughed was a time of celebration for all of them. When she cried, they gathered around her, crooning to her, petting her with loving pats and making funny faces to chase those tears away. "Someone must always hold her, carry her on their back, sleep with her cradled in their arms," Grandmother told them over and over. "She must feel the touch of someone alive and warm, someone who cares."

Em remembered the hospital and orphan babies who lay in rows with clean bandages and food, almost always enough to keep life in them, and yet they lay there with still bodies and eyes that saw nothing, looked at nothing, and had no hope. Perhaps, Em thought, if there had been enough people to love them, as well as feed them and dress their wounds, they now would be like Sami-two. He took her with him to ride and pat his buffalo.

Gradually Sami-two's night agonies grew further apart and lasted a shorter time, but they never stopped completely. Sami-two was getting fat and pretty with a peach glow under her golden skin. She recognized all of them with happy little crows of laughter. But Grandmother, Thu, and Em knew something no one else seemed to notice. Sami-two could not sit up without a propping at her back. She could not move her fat little legs or tiny pink feet. She could neither crawl nor walk. Grandmother and Thu spent hours rubbing her legs and back with sweet-smelling oils and perfumed water. Nothing helped. They knew in their hearts that she never would walk or skip or run like the other children in the hamlet. Grandmother and Thu shared their fear as they shared the baby, Em thought—as they shared everything else, these two, one so old and one so young, and both so alike.

Suddenly it was time for first harvest. The paddy fields

were golden, each breath of air was like a drop of honey on the tongue. Each homestead, each footpath and spur road was filled with activity. At harvesttime everyone works. The fields were full of young and old, men, women, and girls and boys as young as five or six years.

Then Sam came, bringing Father and Chi-Bah in a borrowed army jeep. The two boys, now soldiers in the army, could not come. They were needed to fight, not to harvest a rice crop. Sam and Father could stay three days. Chi-Bah said, "I must go back with them. It would not be safe for me to travel the road alone. Besides . . ." She hesitated, wiping the tears from her face. "Please, Mother, understand. I know the rice must be harvested quickly. I know each family member is needed and expected to work in the fields. I know this, but also I know something else. My husband's destiny and mine take different roads. At least for a time. Perhaps I have Old Uncle's ability to read the stars. I do not know. I know only there is separation ahead for us. I must be near him as long as destiny permits it. My Mother, do you understand?"

Her mother put her arms around the shaking shoulders of her firstborn girl. "I understand. You must go with your father and Sam, but also, my child, you must learn from your father to accept what must be accepted."

"I'll try, Mother," Chi-Bah answered, "but I am not as good as you are."

"You will be," her mother told her, "when life disciplines you as it has disciplined me." Chi-Bah continued to cry. She could not stop.

In the fields everyone was working. First the rice must

be reaped. Grandfather insisted that the old-fashioned sickle be used. There was a newer, better one, Father thought, but he obeyed the man in charge, his father. The stalks were cut as near the base as possible and carried on the backs of the workers to the house, where they were laid on the ground to sun and dry. Then Thu, with Sami-two on her back, raked the stalks, turning them to sun. Paddy was carried in to be stored in one of the rooms in the house. The straw left in the field was collected and carried to the house yard to be dried.

When all the workers left the field, the gleaners took over. This year there were three old women who had no kin left in the hamlet and two small girls. They were careful and thorough workers and picked each small grain they found as tenderly as if it were a precious gem. To them each grain was a precious gem that would fill their empty rice bowls.

After the reaping came the threshing. Here again Grandfather used the method of thirty years ago, when he was considered one of the best young rice-growers of the Mekong delta. He intended to use Em's buffalo; tied to a stake, the buffalo would walk in circles over the stalks, releasing the rice grains. His son in late years had used a rented threshing machine, but even he admitted that threshing with a buffalo softened the stalk fiber and made it better for fodder. Grandfather had not expected an argument with Em. In his young days no one would ever have argued with a grandfather or a father. When Grandfather said he intended to stake the buffalo, Em said, "No, I will talk to him, guiding him with my hand. He has never been prodded." Em could see that Grandfather was displeased. No one had ever argued with him before, and suddenly Grandfather looked old and tired, too tired to argue about whether a buffalo should be prodded or not. Em had his way of walking with his buffalo, and sometimes he rode on the buffalo's back and played his flute. "Because," he told his grandfather, "my buffalo likes my music." The animal seemed to like it when it was grazing near the swamp or the jungle, Grandfather admitted reluctantly. Another thing Em insisted on was a long rest in midmorning and no work in the heat of the day. It took threshing a longer time, but Em was reasonable in his argument. He said, "Except for Sam, this buffalo is my best friend, and this is the way I treat my best friends." Grandfather shrugged but did not object.

Em knew that although the old man was annoyed, Old Uncle was amused. He himself had never dared argue with his own grandfather. Mother, Em sensed, was grateful that he loved his buffalo so much that he would do what he thought was right for it. Anh-Hai, the Elder Son, would not have argued about it, but he was different from Em. He was a serious, quiet boy, obedient and thoughtful in his ways. Perhaps, Mother thought, they had placed the responsibility of being the oldest son too soon on shoulders too young to carry the burden lightly. Anh-Hai always went along with decisions, he never argued.

After the rice was threshed, it was winnowed. Mother and Thu did the winnowing. Standing on sturdy tree stumps, holding the rice-filled baskets on their hips, they slowly spilled it in little rivers of grain to the mats on the ground made to receive it. At this time of year there was always a small wind that blew the chaff from the rice as it was falling to the ground. The mounds of rice on the mats would be cleaned of chaff and all debris. Clean rice was a matter of pride to the delta people.

As a rule the rice that was to be sold would be measured after winnowing, but this year's rice would not be taken to a rice merchant. This year's harvest was small because there had been so few to work in the paddy fields. All they had grown would be needed for the family food supply.

Now that the rice was clean, it was ready to be stored in large, tight reed bins with heavy lids and placed on boards so the dampness of the ground could not seep into the bins and mildew the rice.

The family was satisfied with its labor. There would be no lack of rice before the next harvest. There was a day of prayer and sacrifice offered to the Spirits of the Field, and family feasting. The grueling work of harvest was over.

But there was no time for resting in the shade of the bamboo hedges, or for all-day swimming parties in the waterways and the river. The most important festival of the entire year would take place in three or four weeks' time, and there was much work to be done. This festival would last for seven days, and everyone came home for it. People who had lived in Saigon for years and had forgotten their village ways suddenly remembered them and came back to the hamlet of their childhood and for a week were people of the soil again. Even the military were excused from the business of war for the blessing of peace.

This festival was known as *Têt*. It was a farewell to the

year that had passed and a welcome to the new year. It was a farewell to the House Spirit who ascended to heaven to make his report to the Emperor of Jade on the year's behavior of his family. It was a welcome to the Spirits of the Ancestors who would come back for a few days to the homes they had known in their lifetime.

There was much work to be done in preparation for this festival. First the hamlet was cleaned. The hedges were trimmed and thinned. The gardens were raked and recovered with earth. The windblown leaves and dead and broken branches were carried away. The houses were refreshed and repaired. The pagodas and *dinh* and shrines were cleaned; the tombs were whitewashed, even those of families long since gone from the hamlet. The remains of houses that had been bombed were carried away, and the earth where they had stood smoothed over.

Fresh earth was put in the Chinese pots that made the flower gardens of the houses, and when everything out-of-doors had been done, attention was put to decorating the inside of the houses. The house posts were wrapped in gay colored cloth. Red and yellow banners with Vietnamese characters printed on them were hung from the rafters. Posters decorated the woven mat partitions. There were panels of silk with pictures or designs painted on them. These were ancient and prized possessions. Em's house had only a few.

Many men were poets, some of them quite good, and Old Uncle was the best of all, if what the people thought and said was true. These poems, written in either the classical language, which was very difficult, or the common language of the people, were also part of the house decorations, painted in black or red on the finest rice paper. They were delicate additions to the flamboyant posters and banners.

Flowers of every shape and color filled the bronze pots on the altars and the clay pots on the floor. Bananas were picked in bunches—red ones, long black ones, thin yellow ones, and the *chuoi man*—fat little fingers of gold as sweet as honey. With the bananas were the orange-colored *sapoti* and the ruby-red chili peppers.

At dusk Sam came in an army jeep with Anh-Hai and Chi-Bah's husband, Sinh. The back of the jeep was filled with oranges, grapefruit, limes, tangerines, and mangoes. These were fruits that had to be bought in the market at Cholon and were very expensive, but they made beautiful color combinations with the other fruits and flowers. After excited cries of admiration for Sam's extravagant gifts, and tender welcome to the three young men, a great clamor began. Where were Father and Chi-Bah, and when were they coming? "Father is coming," Anh-Hai told his mother. "The major is coming with him. Although he was born in Saigon, he wants to be a member of our family for *Tết*."

"That is good. That is good," Mother answered, "but where is my little daughter? Where is my Chi-Bah?"

"She is coming with Father and the major," Anh-Hai said.

Sam said, "Let's get this stuff out of the trunk before some low-flying bomber takes a shot at it because he thinks it moved."

Everyone laughed and began carrying the fruit into the house. Em was delighted. "First we will use them to help decorate the house," he said, "and for the feast we will eat them."

"You are as greedy as Sami-two," Thu told him, pushing the baby around to her back to have her arms free to carry in the grapefruit, because she knew where she wanted to pile them on the floor.

After Anh-Hai and Sinh and Sam had been properly thanked, they had to see Sami-two, how rosy and fat she was, how pretty and charming. Only Sam noticed that she could not move her legs and feet. He stood a long time looking at them, touching them gently. Then he said rather than asked, "She makes no effort to walk."

Thu said, "No," but Grandmother was loud in her insistence that she was "merely slow."

"There is something wrong, I think," Sam said gravely. "I wish I had her in the States. I know a doctor—at least I've met him a couple of times—in one of the children's hospitals."

"You could take Sami-two and me to the States," Thu said. "Remember you said you wanted to take me to your mother in Washington."

Sam said, "I'd like that very much, Little Butterfly, but at this time it would be impossible. I'll contact this doctor. Perhaps he can come here."

Thu was satisfied with this, although for a moment she had pictured herself with Sami-two on her back, walking in the streets of Washington, America. Mother was doubtful. "Even if this doctor can come," she said, "would our hospitals have the equipment to make the poor little one's legs work?"

"I don't know," Sam answered, "but I'll write to him."

"And come tell us what he says?" Thu asked anxiously.

"Of course, Little Butterfly," Sam answered teasingly. "Remember Sami-two is mine. I found her first."

"But I'm here to love her the most," Thu said laughingly. She liked being teased by Sam; all the family loved Sam, and their smiling faces showed their love.

Just then the major's car came gliding over the grass with its horn tooting its own welcome. There were more embraces and glad cries of welcome. Grandmother, hugging Chi-Bah, said teasingly, "So the army jeep isn't good enough for the major's secretary!"

Chi-Bah laughed. "What would you have me do? Sit on the grapefruit? Besides, under the seat of the jeep were bundles and bundles of firecrackers."

Old Uncle abruptly left the room. "He's gone out to count the stars." Thu laughed as she said it. She always laughed at Old Uncle and the messages the stars gave him, but Chi-Bah said sharply, "He's gone out to read the stars, and I believe what they tell him." The family looked at her with approval. It was right to believe that each person had his own star that could foretell his destiny. "Thu talks too much," Chi-Bah said, having been made bold by her family's evident approval.

Mother said mildly, "Both my daughters are good girls and live lovingly together. Life will teach them many things they do not know now at this hour." Em saw the girls look at their mother with tenderness. She was so good, so wise. Then they smiled at each other to show their mother they understood.

Nine

EVERYTHING WAS READY for *Têt*. The rice cakes were made and wrapped in banana skins. The sweet soybean soup was simmering on the three stones that made the stove. All the tables in the house were filled with the special foods that were prepared for this much-loved festival.

Today was the twenty-third day of the lunar month, the day Ong Tao, the House Spirit, would go up into the heavens to report to the Emperor of Jade on the family's behavior throughout the year that had just passed. Em, the young one, had painted on red paper a huge carp for Ong Tao to ride as he went into heaven. Em hoped his painting would remind Ong Tao that although he, his grandmother's favorite grandchild, perhaps had not always been a good boy, at least he had tried.

"Maybe you should print what it is supposed to be," Sam said, "so he will know what he is riding on."

"He'll know," Mother said, smiling at her younger son.

"Of course he will know," Grandmother said. "What is it?"

"A carp," Em told her indignantly.

Grandfather placed a bowl of rice on Ong Tao's altar, which, although it was not as large as the Altar of the Ancestors, was just as beautiful. There were no joss sticks burning on it. None burned there while the House Spirit was gone.

Then the family recited their prayers. Em remembered that his prayer had been for a good report to be given about him. Ong Tao was very powerful. He could change the destiny of the family, but he was fair and just and no one feared him.

After the long prayers had been said, the family sat on the mats in front of the Altar and ate rice cakes and sweet soybean soup.

The next day was a quiet one. Everyone was a little worried about the report that was being made. Anh-Hai wrote a poem about the report, making a funny list of each one's faults. It was not a very good poem, but it was full of laughter. The family was delighted that the quiet one, the very sensitive Elder Brother, was learning that life, though it might be difficult and dangerous, could also be fun. They believed in laughter. They thought laughter helped to keep harmony in the home, and harmony brought well-being to the people. Mother put the poem above Ong Tao's altar. Ong Tao would like it. That's why the family liked him: he reported on them, but he did it with laughter. Although he might worry them, he never humiliated them, and they were grateful. Em remembered now that he had thought, Next year I'll write a poem to Ong Tao, and perhaps Mother will hang it beside Anh-Hai's poem.

On the seventh morning of *Têt* Sam helped prepare the symbolic tree, for on that day, seven days after the departure of Ong Tao to make his report, he would return to his own house bringing with him all the Spirits of the Ancestors who belonged to the house and its family. Grandfather was not certain that Sam should have a hand in preparing the tree, but Anh-Hai said, "I have a feeling that Sam's destiny is part of ours. Why does he stay here and not go back to America, where everyone knows he wants to be? It's his destiny, I tell you. Let him help prepare the tree."

No one was convinced. They thought the argument should be much stronger, but they were so surprised and pleased that Anh-Hai should speak up about what he thought was right that everyone agreed that Sam should help prepare for *Têt*. Even Grandfather said, aside to Father, "There may be something to the boy that we have not noticed before."

Father agreed. "The army is making a man of him!"

But Grandfather said, "No! Nothing about the army or war helps anyone. They destroy. The boy has followed the good example I set for him. And the one I set for you," Grandfather added.

In front of the entrance to Em's home and to most of

the other houses in the hamlet a bamboo pole was planted. Anh-Hai and Em had selected the pole and brought it in and planted it in the spot Old Uncle indicated would be right. The pole was decorated with bamboo branches. On the branches were hung tiny articles made of votive paper. These articles were carefully saved from year to year, and some of them were very old. Em remembered that on the branches of the pole were a tiny paper horse, a circular hat, boots, and a cape—all the things Ong Tao would need to take with him on his trip to heaven. There was also a charm made of straw—a perfect star and very beautiful. The boy wondered if Old Uncle had made it or if it had been in the family for many years, but in the excitement of decorating the pole he had never asked. Grandfather tied a small woven basket of salt to one of the branches, and Father tied a basket of rice. Old Uncle was the last to hang something on the tree—a finger-size basket that had been made waterproof by varnishing it with resin from one of the jungle trees.

"It looks something like our Christmas tree," Sam said. "Does it have a meaning?"

Old Uncle answered him. "Yes. It is to frighten evil spirits away from our house during the visit the Spirits of the Ancestors will honor us with tomorrow."

"But some houses do not have a pole," Sam said. "I wonder why."

Old Uncle answered sadly, "There are Vietnamese who do not believe in some of our ancient traditions, which is bad for our future. We are an ancient people and in our traditions lies our strength."

Grandfather, Father, and Anh-Hai lighted the joss

sticks on the Altar of the Ancestors. Em remembered it now—the perfume of flowers, the blue smoke from the shavings of aloe wood burning in the perfume pot, the waxy smell of candles, the heavy silence of awe and reverence, and the members of his family bowing before the Altar and reciting prayers. It was a blending of colors and fragrances and sounds that would live in his heart forever. Such a *Tết* would never be again, he thought. What had made it was gone.

The day passed quietly, like a calm sea at noontime, with the hours like gentle waves breaking in foam against the seawall of time.

In the early evening the calmness was shattered by firecrackers being set off from time to time, but not too many at one time and not too often. No one had an oversupply of firecrackers, and most of them had to be saved until midnight when even the stars trembled from the sparkle and noise of exploding fireworks.

At midnight the men put on the traditional and treasured ceremonial clothes that were kept through the decades for the festival of *Tết*. Grandfather made an offering of food and burned votive paper on the Altar of the Ancestors, and each member of the family, including Sam, the major, and Sami-two, carried by Thu, took a burning joss stick and bowed low before the Altar. The ancestors would know they were welcome.

Then a *Tết* meal of many special *Tết* foods was eaten, and the prayers were repeated until dawn of the new day, when the pole was taken down and its decorations put away. Em remembered taking them down, helping his Grandmother put them away, so carefully—so carefully.

"These are getting very old. They must last at least for one more *Têt*," she had said.

"Even if they do not last," Old Uncle answered, "there will always be the memory of this *Têt*."

"It has been a very special *Têt*," Chi-Bah said softly.

Soon they were gone, Chi-Bah riding in the major's car, which Father was driving, and the two young Vietnamese soldiers riding with Sam in the borrowed U. S. Army jeep. "If Elder Sister wants to be near her husband," Em asked Thu, "why doesn't he ride with her in the major's car?"

Thu was horrified. "They are just soldiers. The major is an officer. Soldiers do not ride in officers' cars."

"I don't understand why," Em grumbled.

"It's a rule," Thu said in a grown-up voice which she now used when she remembered to do so.

Em went out with his buffalo. "You are so much easier to understand, my friend," he had said to it.

Time passed. Trying to remember now how long it had been, Em could not. The time was between *Têt* and rice-planting season, he knew, but this year the pattern seemed to be broken. In other years between February and May the days had been full of activity. "We must do this before rice planting." Or, "These things must be done before rice planting," they had said every day. This year there had been little talk about rice planting.

"I must start planning." Grandfather fretted.

"Too early, wait awhile," Old Uncle replied.

Grandfather said, "We should be examining the tools and getting them in shape for planting."

"Wait until the signs are right," Old Uncle answered.

Every day Thu would ask Old Uncle if Sam would come with news of the doctor who would examine Sami-two. Old Uncle would answer crossly, "How can I know about Sam? His star isn't in the sky of Vietnam. I like Americans, but I doubt if they have stars that hold their destiny."

Em asked Old Uncle to continue teaching him. Old Uncle refused. "Have you taught me all I can learn from you?" Em asked, hurt by his uncle's refusal.

"You must learn new things of which I have no knowledge," the old man said sadly.

"You can teach me the harvest songs that I did not know last harvest. You have knowledge of those," Em said.

Grandfather laughed—something he had not done in weeks. "The best harvest songs are the ones you make up. When we were young, those were the good days. All the boys would go in one group and the girls would go in another group to the hamlet well by the *dinh*. We'd go to carry back the house supply of water, but if the harvest moon was full, we'd sing. Remember those days and the songs we made up?" Grandfather said, looking at Grandmother, who did not look at him. The old man laughed again, poking his finger at Grandmother.

"No," she answered primly, but in the next breath, "Do you remember the first one you sang to me?"

Grandfather thought awhile. Then he said, "I can tell you," and then he sang, "Pretty girl, can you tell me, can you tell me, how many stars there are in the sky?" Then he sang, mimicking Grandmother's voice, "I can tell you, I can tell you, if you can count all the hairs in my head."

Everyone laughed but Em, who was horrified. "Why, Grandfather! You couldn't do that. Boys and girls are not supposed to touch each other. How could you count the hairs on Grandmother's head?"

Everyone laughed again. "That's the point," Grandfather said, still laughing. "It shows you aren't old enough to sing the harvest songs."

Em thought a bit, then he sang, trying to mimic Thu's voice, "Can you tell me, can you tell me, how many fish there are in the sea?" Then in his own voice, "I can tell you, I can tell you if you can count my fingers and toes."

"That isn't any good," Thu said. "Everyone *knows* you have ten fingers and ten toes. They wouldn't have to count them—they know." She used her new grown-up voice.

The argument that was about to follow was stopped by the roar of a motorcycle. "It's Sam! It's Sam!" Em shouted, and everyone went outside to welcome him. Sam stopped his motor and staggered, rather than walked, into the house. "Are you hurt?" Mother asked.

"Sit here on the mat," Grandmother said. "I will bring you hot tea."

Sam sat on the mat, his hands covering his face. Mother asked again, "Are you hurt, Sam? Tell us."

Grandmother came back with the tea, which she held to his mouth as she would have done for Sami-two. Thu whispered, "Is it that the doctor won't come to see Sami-two?"

Sam shook his head; he began to look better now that he had sipped the tea Grandmother held for him.

"The doctor is coming? When? Tomorrow?"

Sam smiled, although his face was still white and strained. "Not tomorrow, Little Butterfly. He says the team he is coming with will get here in about six weeks, but I would say three months. These things move slowly, but he will come, I hope, and he will know what can be done for Sami-two."

"Sam," was all that Thu could say. Grandmother held the tea again to Sam's mouth and Sam sipped it gratefully.

Old Uncle said, "Tell them why you came, Sam. I would have told them, but they only partly believe what my stars tell me."

"Is it about Chi-Bah?" Mother asked in a whisper. "Is it about my Number One Daughter?"

Sam looked at her without speaking.

"Tell them what happened first," Old Uncle advised, "and then what happened next so they will not be confused. Talk slowly, Sam, giving each event its proper moment so it will be engraved in their hearts forever."

The old man's words seemed to bring Sam back to reality. Em could see Sam's face in his memory. Sam had closed his eyes. Em knew Sam was here to tell this family—who were really his Number Two Family—something that would break their hearts.

"Tell them what happened first," Old Uncle repeated.

"Well, first," Sam said, and he seemed surprised that his words were so steady, "Chi-Bah heard the rumor that Saigon was going to fall, that America had offered refuge to all who were loyal to their government and had been friendly and helpful to all the Americans."

"Saigon falling!" Mother interrupted. "That could

never happen. The French built Saigon to last."

Sam did not seem to have heard her and continued talking. "The American families living in Saigon and the Vietnamese civilians were frantic to get any ship or plane that would get them to America. Some were even using fishing boats. Poor Chi-Bah was frightened. She went to her husband's camp to ask him what she should do, how could she save her family." Sam pushed the bowl of tea away. What he had to say must be said quickly. He was not like Old Uncle, Em thought. He was an American who had to get things done neatly and quickly. He continued talking. "When she arrived at the camp, she could not find either her husband or her brother. 'Gone,' a Vietnamese guard told her. 'Where?' 'I don't know, maybe fighting someplace, maybe taken prisoner, maybe dead. I don't know what happens in this war.' "

Sam gulped another scalding swallow of the tea which Grandmother so patiently held out to him. "When she went to find her father, the palace had been bombed," he said flatly.

Grandfather began lighting the joss sticks on the Altar. Old Uncle lighted the candles and put perfume in the perfume pans. Mother sobbed, "Where is my little girl? What happened to her?"

"She is all right," Sam said. "I found her not far from Cholon, trying to walk home to you. I took her back to the hospital. She was in shock."

"Tell it all," Old Uncle repeated, and his voice was quiet and firm.

Em crept closer to Sam, and Thu and Sami-two took refuge in Grandmother's arms. Only Mother stood idle, looking at Sam. "And her father was killed when they bombed the palace," she stated rather than asked. "Did Chi-Bah know it?"

Sam nodded.

Grandfather passed the burning joss around. "My husband is dead," Mother said, as if trying to believe what she was saying. "My son, my son," Grandmother wept. Grandfather turned to look at them.

"His body is dead," he told them, "but his spirit is with us to guide us, to protect us, to love us."

The family bowed before the Altar of the Ancestors, even Sam, with the joss sticks in one hand and his other arm around Em, who had neither spoken nor cried.

Ten

IT WAS TIME to take his buffalo home for the noontime rest. Already the midday heat was pushing down from the heavens, but Em remembered that he had not wanted to go home. There was harmony in his house and more love than he had ever remembered. Father always had said, "When there is harmony in the home, there is love, and this brings well-being to the family." But there was no happiness. Grandmother and Thu worked daily with Sami-two, who had become a creature of laughter. She could talk now, and they could understand a few of the many words of jabber she poured out continuously. She could make them laugh, but it was only halfhearted laughter, trying to show her that they loved her. She could not walk.

Grandfather prayed endlessly by the Altar of the Ancestors, burning joss and perfume oil and candles when someone brought them from Cholon. He did nothing but pray.

At first Old Uncle had said to Em, "Your father would want us to sharpen the plow, to put a new rake on the harrow, to see if the paddle wheel works," but Old Uncle did not know how to do these things, and Em could only help and could not do them alone. Old Uncle gave up. He said, "War has no need of a man of books, only one of violence."

Em wanted Sam to come. Sam always knew what to do. Mother wanted Sam to come. He had promised to bring Chi-Bah home as soon as she was able to travel. Thu wanted Sam to come and to bring the promised doctor. But Sam did not come.

When Old Uncle realized that he did not know how to mend the tools, nor did he know how to plan for rice planting, he left the house more often and stayed away for longer times. When Mother told her younger son to find Old Uncle and coax him to come home to eat, sometimes the old man did come home, but all the time he was home he kept saying, "Saigon is falling. Our world that we have known is coming to an end."

Now Em stopped writing. He looked with surprise at his hands that were wet with perspiration, and he felt it on his forehead, stinging his eyes. He looked at his hands for a long time, then wiped the sweat from his face, wondering why it wasn't blood he was seeing, his own blood, for he felt he was bleeding inside. He had come to the time he had dreaded. "If this is to be a record to give to those who follow me, it must be a record in truth. I must write each part as it happened, when it happened," he said aloud. No one answered him, although he could see his thin little grandmother bowing low before the Altar and shaking so violently that Em watched in fear that she would fall. Elder Sister sobbed, but Em knew it was for her own heartbreak. The boy went to the Altar of the Ancestors and bowed before it; then he turned back to the table. He was head of this family. He must be the example. What had happened had happened. Nothing could change it. The events of the world move, but they move forward. It was his task to write of the past.

He sat again at the table and willed himself to remember, every sight, every sound, every smell, every word that had been said.

But he realized he was confused about the time. How many weeks had his father been taken from them when this day happened? he wondered. But time did not matter. What month it was or week—he remembered the day. "I will write it as it happened from hour to hour. That will bring me to the moment," he said aloud.

Old Uncle said, "The truth must be written."

Em looked at the old man in surprise. This was the first time he had known Old Uncle to be aware of what was going on around him when he was in meditation. Em did not answer. Closing his eyes, he began to bring his memory, clear and precise, back to that day.

He had taken his buffalo to a shady, hidden cove, to stand belly-high in the water and let the birds clean its itching back of insects. Most times Em swam with his buffalo, but today he lay on the great creature's back and played his flute, not knowing or caring if it was a song Old Uncle had taught him or one he was making up. Suddenly the buffalo became uneasy. Em also had a sudden desire to go home. He felt his buffalo's flesh quiver beneath his body. He watched the buffalo toss its head and increase, a little, its usual steady but slow speed.

They went out of the cove and through the forest, where the trees thinned and the sky could be seen. Far above them, small dots in the blue of the sky, the bombers flew in formation. Today the boy had not heard their roar, or had heard it without noticing. When they reached the edges of the swamp, the buffalo became more uneasy. Em, too, felt fear and smelled something he could not name. Was it burning bamboo logs? Were they burning the dead plants in the field as they sometimes did at this time of year? Then he smelled smoke; he could taste smoke; it choked his throat and his nostrils; it burned his eyes until he could hardly see. This was smoke, but what had caused it?

When he cleared the edges of the swamp, he saw where the smoke came from.

The hamlet where he had lived all of his life, where his family lived, was gone. It was not there any more. There were a few felled and still burning trees. There was an American bulldozer leveling the ground, turning over the earth to cover the debris. There was a handful of hamlet people, and there were Vietnamese soldiers and Americans everywhere.

Em rode his buffalo to the place where his house had

been standing this morning when he had left it to take the animal to graze. "What have you done to my house?" he yelled in shock and fury. "Where is my family?"

"The kid speaks English," an American beside him said. Em thought he was a captain, but he was not sure.

Then he saw Sam, but this was not the quiet, gentle man he had known. This man was a wild man, hitting American and Vietnamese soldiers alike, yelling at them. The captain shouted to his men, "Don't shoot him. He's only a reporter gone crazy because he saw a family he knew killed."

"Bombed!" Sam shouted back. "Why don't you say the word? They were bombed, blown to bits, not a whole body left. Oh, my God, why do you let this happen?"

Then Sam saw Em riding his buffalo. He ran to him in the smoke and confusion.

"Sam!" Sam was there. Em thought, he will make this bad dream go away. "It was a mistake, Em," Sam said brokenly. "It's easy to miss your mark. These villages all look alike."

The American captain said in disgust, "Sam, you're getting soft. You know this place was full of VC's. These people know the VC's will torture them and eventually kill them, and yet they feed them. They shelter them. Don't tell me this hamlet wasn't full of VC's."

"There were none in my family. My family was loyal to our government and friendly to the United States," Em told him.

"Well, get off that buffalo and get your family together and start moving. We're taking you to the refugee camp," the soldier answered.

"I won't go to the camp," Em said. Still in shock, he clung to his buffalo. "I won't move from here. I won't get off this buffalo. My father told me this buffalo was my responsibility, and I'm staying with it."

"Look, kid," the captain said, trying to reason with him. "This place isn't safe. Your buffalo has to be shot and bulldozed under. That young giant would feed a VC gang for a week."

"I won't get off. I won't move him," Em had said.

Tears came to Em's eyes now as he remembered the events that followed. Sam, who had been listening to Em and the American, started to speak, but then leaped forward in an attempt to grab Em. He pulled Em from the buffalo, and Em fell to the ground as the shots rang out. The buffalo fell, and when Em looked, he saw his buffalo on the ground and Sam lying across it. Em tried to go to him, but the soldiers held him. "He's gone," they told him in Vietnamese. "Both dead. Too bad."

Now that the American captain's order had been obeyed, he seemed to go insane. "Sam," he shouted, "I didn't mean it for you! Sam, my God! Why did you rush in!" The captain turned to Em. "Sam and I went to school together, and then before my eyes he kills himself."

"He didn't kill himself," Em shouted, in tears. "He went in to save me and my friend, my buffalo. You killed him."

This seemed to upset the captain even more. "This war is making us all crazy," the captain said, almost to himself. "We don't know what we're doing." He turned away and in a moment was barking further orders. "Get that old woman over here, the one carrying the pot bigger than she is."

Em turned to see his grandmother stumbling toward him through the smoke and rubble. He held out his arms.

"Good," the captain said. "That's two we've got that belong together. Who is the old man, the one near her? What's he carrying?"

"What does the beast say?" Grandmother asked Em.

"He wants to know what Old Uncle is carrying."

"He's carrying our record Book of Ancestors, and no one is to take it from him," Grandmother answered.

"What does the old woman say?" the captain asked.

"It's a book he likes," Em answered.

The captain said to the Vietnamese soldiers beside him, "Put him on a litter and get him to the camp. I don't think he'll make it, but let him keep his book." Then the captain told Em, "There was another old man with the old woman. Ask her where he went."

"Tell him," Grandmother answered, "he went into the tunnel when our house started to burn. Tell him this land was his to take care of for his children and his children's children. Tell him they can't make him leave it now."

"She says," Em said, trying not to think about what her words meant, "he was our grandfather. He went somewhere."

Grandmother said, crying, "I still have Old Uncle, and I still have you. Your mother," she said, pointing to the bulldozer leveling the land, "Thu, and little Sami-two are there together. Their spirits will be at rest. Your grandfather will never be back. He went into the tunnel that be-longed to his land."

"And Sam and my buffalo are here, too," Em said, but he did not cry.

Em remembered they had no trouble in strapping Old Uncle in the litter. "Let me keep my book," he said again and again. He did not seem to know or care what hap-pened. Grandmother refused the litter. She refused to let anyone but Em carry the huge clay pot. "Did Chi-Bah come with . . ." He could not finish the question, but his Grandmother did it for him: "With Sam? No. He said he could not find her, and when he heard about this hamlet he came at once. He was trying to keep us together, your grandfather, your mother, Old Uncle, Thu and Sami-two and me. We and Chi-Bah were all that were left, he said. Then he saw you and ran to you, and Grandfather went into the tunnel. I saw him go." After a minute of silence she asked, "Where is this refugee camp? Can we find Chi-Bah?"

"I don't know, Grandmother. I don't know what we can do without Sam."

Grandmother took his hand. They walked the rest of the way in silence.

There were only about twenty in the group, all that were left of the little hamlet. Some were crying, a few were moaning in pain, but most of the group were silent. When would the war be over? When would peace come again? What would happen to the handful that were left? No one knew.

Eleven

ALTHOUGH THE REFUGEE CAMP was less than twenty miles away, it was very different from their flower-filled grassy hamlet hedged with bamboo, bounded by rivers, swampland, and jungle. Here in this new place there were no canals, no mighty river, no flowering fruit trees—only barren, rocky soil enclosed by barbed-wire fences. Inside the wire enclosure were shacks made from sheets of tin. There was no shade, only the blazing sun sweeping over and through the tin roofs and walls.

The refugees were not ill-treated; they were given water and food, and vegetable seeds for planting, although the soil was too poor to nourish the plants and there was no water for irrigation. Em and the others sat in their hut for days. There were other refugees there from their own hamlet, but Em did not know how or where to find them.

The food that was given them was not much and not to their liking, but it was enough for existence. Old Uncle ate. He seemed to be out of shock, although he complained that he could not see well, and he was confused about where he was and why he was there. He kept asking for Sam, saying Sam had promised to take him to America and that he was ready to go.

Grandmother was very frightened. She kept her head and face covered, hoping perhaps that if she could not see, she could not be seen, but she always kept a hand on her clay pot and the record Book of Ancestors that Old Uncle had held in his arms. Grandmother remembered everything and kept reciting it as a litany over and over and over. Grandmother would not eat—she slept fitfully.

Now Em knew what Sam never could have told him. Thinking back now, Em could not remember what he had done or how he had felt. He knew he had not cried. He had not been hungry. He did not remember having slept. He thought he had just sat there waiting for nothing, now that his mother and Sam and his buffalo had gone. Sometimes he thought it had not happened; it was a dream and he would waken, but he never did.

A week went by, perhaps a month—Em could not remember—but one stifling afternoon Chi-Bah came with the officer who had ordered the buffalo shot and who had killed Sam, too. Even before he saw Chi-Bah, Old Uncle recognized the officer, although he had been insisting he could not see. At his cry Grandmother uncovered her face. "You murderer!" she cried in Vietnamese, and then, seeing Chi-Bah, said, "My poor little dear one, leave this man at once. He is evil."

Chi-Bah knelt by her grandmother, cradling her as if she had been Sami-two who had been hurt.

Em remembered that he and Old Uncle had said nothing. They had just sat there looking at the evil man Chi-Bah had brought to them. "Old Uncle, Grandmother, Em," the girl pleaded, "listen to me. This man's name is John. He found me standing on a street corner. The hospital had discharged me. There were dozens waiting for my cot. The roads out of Saigon were blocked. I had no place to go."

The three people listened to her but did not speak.

Chi-Bah was still talking. "This man, John, told me what happened at the hamlet. He thought the bombing had been a mistaken mark, but maybe not, he said. There were VC's everywhere. He told me what he had done to Em's buffalo and to Sam. 'Sam was my best friend,' he said. 'We grew up together, went to school together, dated girls together.' The buffalo had to be shot and bulldozed under, or it would have added to the VC food supply and the VC strength."

The American's face appealed to them for understanding. "All wars are insane," John said, shaking his head.

"He spoke the truth there," Old Uncle said. "But what bothers me is how he knew you."

Chi-Bah answered simply, "He saw Sam with us. He knew all of us. He said the fellows used to tease Sam about his Vietnamese family."

Old Uncle became confused. "Where is Sam?" he

complained. "He promised to take me to America, and I am ready to go." No one answered him. He would neither understand nor accept their explanation.

"Have you finished talking?" Grandmother asked.

"No," Chi-Bah answered. "John has been looking for me for a week because he knew that was what Sam would want him to do." Chi-Bah began to cry. No one comforted her.

Old Uncle spoke again, but in his normal, shaky voice. "What's done is done. Who knows but that all this is what was meant to be. Who has ever read each word in the Book of Heaven?"

Grandmother, hearing Uncle speak in a normal way, now found the strength to speak. "What does this evil man want?" she asked. "To kill the rest of us?"

Chi-Bah stood up, her face flaming with anger. "He came to find me, and then he hunted until we found you. And there is something else." Her voice quavered. "Anh-Hai is dead."

Old Uncle said, "So Anh-Hai is dead, like his grandfather and his father, and the young one here is now head of the house." The only sounds in the hut were of the two women crying. The men were silent. Em remembered that he had thought, I don't want to be head of the family. I want everything to be as it used to be.

They all looked at him, expecting him to say something. He said, "I loved Anh-Hai. I didn't want him to die."

Chi-Bah said between sobs, "You couldn't love him as much as I. He was older than I. He carried me on his back until I was almost as big as he was. He always took care of me. I wish he had not had to die."

Em had said loudly, "I don't want to be head of the family. I don't know how to make decisions. I am not old enough."

The old man told him sternly, "You have knowledge— I gave it to you. You are thoughtful. I taught you to meditate. Your ancestors have set the patterns you must follow."

His grandmother had added, "You are to carry on the family line with honor. It has been written in the Book of Heaven."

Twelve

THEY HAD DECIDED to try to go to America.

Now, instead of nothing to think about, the hours were filled with agonizing worry. They had paid the money and had the papers that permitted them to leave Vietnam. But where were they to go? No town in America had asked for them. No American group had promised to sponsor the family after they arrived in America, helping them to find jobs and a house to live in. The people at the refugee camp were cheerful and hopeful. They said, "There will be a town to take you. There will be some group to sponsor you. There will be jobs found for those who can work." However, they said, "There are thousands like you who need to be taken care of. These things take time. Try to be patient."

Old Uncle was worried about Sam. He asked everyone he met, "Do you know where Sam is? Why hasn't he come to get me as he promised?" Most of the people he asked gave no answer at all, hurrying along to wherever they were going. Old Uncle asked Chi-Bah, "Did you mail the letters Sam gave you for his parents? Did you mail them at the right place? Did you do it correctly? Why have we had no answer?"

Chi-Bah, having learned answers from the agencies, would reply, "There are thousands of letters going out daily. This takes time. Try to be patient."

Em had worries too, but, being head of the family, he did not talk about them. This was not for him to do. Grandmother was their only comfort. Again and again she told them, "If it is the Will of Heaven that we go, we go. Learn to accept this."

Then one day the papers came. The family had a town that would accept them. They had a church group that would sponsor and help them. They had their permits and papers and were ready to go, but there was no place available on ship or plane. At first they stood in line, fighting to keep their place, being pushed backward and forward, being separated. At last they found a place to sit in the hot sun, but it was better than standing and being in danger of falling and being trampled on. John and two of his friends took turns keeping their places in the long line.

Then came the day they stepped on the plane. Old

Uncle refused to board, saying he was waiting for Sam. He had to be carried to the seat assigned to him. At last they took off, zooming into the clouds.

The memory was finished. Grandmother looked at the paper. Nothing had been written on it. Perhaps it was as well, but Grandmother had expected something. Suddenly Em wrote an old proverb his father had taught him: "It takes a strong man to stand against the wind." His grandmother pinned the paper on the wall with the other poems. She was very proud.

Em took his place on the mat before the Altar and began to cry.

Bibliography

Bergman, Arlene Eisen. *Women of Viet-Nam.* San Francisco: People Press (2680 21st St., San Francisco, Ca. 94110), 1974.

Buttinger, Joseph. *The Smaller Dragon.* New York: Praeger Publishers, Inc., 1958.

Chagnon, Jacqui, and Luce, Don, comps. and eds. *Of Quiet Courage.* Washington, D.C.: Indochina Mobile Education Project (1322 18th St., N.W., Washington, D.C., 20013), 1974.

Dooley, Thomas A., M.D. *The Night They Burned the*

Mountain. New York: The New American Library, Inc., Signet Books, 1961.

Du, Nguyen. *The Tale of Kieu*. New York: Random House, Inc., 1973.

Fall, Bernard B. *Last Reflections on a War*. Garden City, N.Y.: Doubleday and Company, Inc., Shocken Books, 1972.

————. *The Two Viet-Nams*. New York: Praeger Publishers, Inc., 1966.

Fitzgerald, Frances. *Fire in the Lake*. New York: Random House, Inc., Vintage Books, 1972.

Hickey, Gerald Cannon. *Village in Vietnam*. New Haven, Conn.: Yale University Press, 1964.

Lacouture, Jean. *Viet Nam: Between Two Truces*. New York: Random House, Inc., 1966.

Lifton, Betty Jean, and Fox, Thomas C. *Children of Vietnam*. West Hanover, Mass.: Halliday Lithograph Corporation, 1972.

Merton, Thomas. *New Seeds of Contemplation*. New York: New Directions Publishing Corporation, 1962.

Reps, Paul, comp. *Zen Flesh, Zen Bones*. Garden City, N.Y.: Doubleday and Company, Inc., Anchor Books, 1961.

Thai-Van-Kiem, M.M., and Nguyen-Ngoc-Linh, eds. *Vietnamese Realities*. Saigon, 1969.

Van Hoa Viet Nam, Culture of Viet Nam. New York: Clergy and Laity Concerned (235 East 49th St., New York, N.Y. 10017). A pamphlet.